Sarah Colliver is the author
Still', a two-book series, se.....
mountains. If you enjoy a dramatic, sexy and gritty
storyline, these books are for YOU.

What the readers are saying about 'IN DEEP':

"Really enjoyed this book, I was hooked from the
beginning and couldn't put it down! Went straight
onto the second book!"

"I absolutely love the book! The story was amazing
and I couldn't stop reading as it was so exciting. Soon
as I finished the first one I had to buy the second
one."

"Thoroughly enjoyed this book! With the clever
twists and turns it captured me from start to finish.
I'm looking forward to the 2nd book."

IN DEEP (Book 1)

Can anything good come of a couple brought together by depravity? Will Tate survive Bill's world, as he loses his edge and danger looms over them both? Set beneath the heat of the Spanish sun, and told from perspectives of both main characters, IN DEEP is a fast ride with twists and turns as treacherous as the mountain roads.

BILL'S GREYING temples and fatigue confirm his fears, he is getting too old in the tooth for the drama and games in his world. His confidence and trim physique still command attention, but his once insatiable appetite for women is depleting, and he is wondering how long he can survive the treachery. His quick thinking and empty promises have kept him safe until now, but the dark figure of Tony, his old boss, is watching his every move.

TATE IS full of hope that her future lies with Bill, that he will be able to move on from their 'business arrangement' and realise that he can't live without her. Her life is built on lies and pretence, but she is determined to leave the gutter behind, to enjoy the finer things in life which Bill offers her. It is only a matter of time until he asks her to move in with him, makes their relationship official, and then she can leave her trade firmly in the past.

Will anyone survive, or are they already in too deep?

DEEPER STILL (Book 2)

TATE is young, beautiful and successful. With the past firmly behind her, she is looking towards a bright future. Although a shadowy past funded her lifestyle, she deserves every penny for what she suffered, right?

Ellie is determined to get hold of everything her dad, Bill, had stolen from him, whilst he perished in the fire. It is rightfully hers after all. But she is plagued by demons, and her drug habit feeds her darkness. Her arrival will shake Tate's new life to the core.

This story will sweep you up into the eye of a storm, as you watch the events unfold from both perspectives.
Will anyone survive, as they fall DEEPER STILL?

Both books are available NOW on Amazon, in paperback and on Kindle.

WE CLOSE
OUR EYES

SOMETIMES WE CLOSE OUR EYES,
rather than face the truth and deal with the
consequences.

I dedicate this book to my husband, Steve.

He tirelessly supports me through my health battles,

is my best friend and my constant.

I thank my lucky stars every day, that we found each

other.

SHERRY

As Sherry dragged the last bulging cardboard box, in through the cottage doorway; a clean smell of fresh paint clung in the air. She exhaled and pushed the door shut behind her with her bottom. Her parched throat and weariness begged for coffee, and she began to hunt down her machine. A motorbike roar drew her to the front window, and she craned her neck to look, skilfully avoiding her piles of kitchenware. But the rider was gone before she could even catch a glimpse.

The kitchen was tiny, but perfect. Quaint and quirky, it would not suit everyone, but she loved it even though it was full of boxes filled with items which should have been de-cluttered prior to moving. Perhaps she could sell some stuff at a car boot sale, or on Ebay, it certainly wasn't all going to fit. Even the poor car had groaned with the weight of it all, and she imagined its relief now it stood empty once again.

She rummaged through the carrier bags for fresh coffee and milk and plugged in her machine. The important thing was, that she and her belongings

1

were in, and the door was now closed to her dark past. It already felt like a fresh start, and she had not realised until that exact moment, how much she needed one. A cosy cottage in the country, was something she could have only dreamed of twelve months before. The village consisted of a thatched pub, perfect, she hoped, for cosy Sundays by a roaring fire, and delicious food. A shop which doubled as a post office, a well-stocked butchers and a farm shop. There would be little reason to leave the village at all. Coffee vapours filled her nose and curled her mouth into a smile.

A rusty old key in the kitchen door brought to mind her grandma's house, back when her hair was pulled tightly into pigtails and her socks up to her knees. To the days before, when her behaviour could be attributed to her childish ways or tantrums. When the answer to every troubled 'incident' could be answered with a, 'she'll grow out of it.' Only she had not managed that yet, and adult life was not so forgiving.

An unfamiliar warmth crept across her, which she soon recognised as safety and contentment. Something which was talked about by other people but had escaped her until now. It confirmed that this quaint cottage, along the sparsely housed road, on the edge of the picture-perfect village, was exactly where she should be. With all her planets finally aligned, everything she had gone through, brought her to this spot. She could begin again, create a new persona. Learn to forget.

The key turned easily, despite its weathered shell and she pulled open the creaky door. Lavender, crawling with bees, scented the air as she hopped along the crazy paving path through the grass and shrubs. Above the far end of the garden, a huge canopy of woodland stretched up towards the cloudless sky and promised shade from the predicted heatwave summer. A gate sunk back into the hedge, offered passage into the woods and excitement grew inside her hungry tummy-her own secret garden!

A gentle breeze carried across raised voices and she turned towards them. A gnarled knot hole in the fence, drew her eye towards two figures in the distance- a man and a woman.

"Please don't do this to me, you know I could lose everything!" The woman was a similar age to her, with a high red ponytail and smart white shirt. Sherry glanced down at her own tatty appearance, but dismissed any self-berating on account that it was moving day, and you never look your best on those kinds of days.

His arms folded across his chest as he looked down at her, expressionless. Whilst she seemed amid meltdown, he remained quiet, steely. He was dressed in leathers, perhaps he was the biker she heard arriving before.

"I feel like I'm losing my mind!" She repeatedly smacked her palm against her forehead, and guttural screams escaped her mouth. He did not move, simply stared. "I'm literally begging you now, please tell them there is no more. He is going to find out any time soon, and all hell's gonna break loose. He will end it this time, I know it…"

Guilt momentarily pecked at Sherry for watching, yet she could not look away. As she was hidden from their view, she remained pressed against the rough fence panel.

The woman sank to the floor and grappled at his legs. "Why? Why are you doing this to me? I paid every penny, as instructed, can't you leave me alone now?"

"That was before. You only have yourself to blame. The question is, what is worse – him doing his nut about some cash, or finding out what you did? In fact, the world finding out, not just him. I can't see you have much choice."

Her ashen face and wide eyes resembled a haunting. She shook her head and wailed. "Nooo! He can never, *never* know about that. I think he would kill me..." Her hands clung to his calves, begging for mercy.

"Look at you...what you've become..." He untangled her grasping hands and kicked her away. "You're a mess now. You can't go back to before, not after what you did."

"I wasn't like this until you came along!"

"Hey! Don't be laying that at my door. Remember who you called for help? Remember who came? Well now you're paying the price, and if you ask me, you're getting off bloody lightly."

"You wanted me, once. I was good enough for you then."

He laughed. "You disgust me, you're a joke...the depths you're prepared to stoop...you were a somebody and now... you're not even decent in the sack."

She flew at him and beat his torso with her clenched fists. "You bastard!"

He elongated, and appeared to grow in height as he grabbed her wrists and yanked her close. Sherry could see his tensed shoulders, and imagined his jaw to be clenched, as he whispered something inaudible. The woman stopped struggling and turned to stone. He released his vice-like grip and she wiped down her trousers, lifted her head and walked away.

Sherry gasped, what could he have said? He pushed his hair from his face, and lit up a cigarette, blowing smoke rings up into the air. With a wry smile, he turned and headed out of the thicket, but he flicked his head towards Sherry, and his grey eyes bored into her. Could he see her? Surely not from that distance. Although she stood firm, her wide eyes returned his gaze, and her knees shook. It must be her imagination because there was a hefty old fence between them. Her heartbeat filled the silence. She blinked rapidly, and he was gone.

DAN

"You met the newcomer yet?" Joan's gnarled fingers sifted through her purse of coins.

"Been in once or twice, seemed okay." Dan leaned back against the bread shelves, wondering how long it would take her to find the right money for her eggs and wishing he were at home in the office, tackling the pile of invoices.

"Well, remember, people aren't always what they seem young man, don't you be too trusting. You know that, look at Daisy, here one minute and gone the next."

Dan smiled but his cheeks blushed. "Thanks for the advice, Joan, I promise to bear it in mind." He swiped the coins from the counter and deposited them into the till, without counting them. "See you tomorrow." He yawned.

"Aye, you will, tala." Joan hobbled through the door but stopped still with the rumble of a motorbike, halting in front of her. "You bikers, send me to an early grave you will!" She lifted her stick and shook it towards the unsuspecting biker, who swiftly took her

7

by the arm and forcefully crossed her over the road before marching into the shop.

"What's her beef?" The biker tipped his head towards Joan, who angrily waved her walking stick in the air and shouted inaudible insults.

"She doesn't live that side of the road, livid she is. What can I get you?" Dan's face twitched.

"Cigarettes? You got any?"

"Sorry mate, no, we don't sell them in here, we're a farm shop. But around the corner, the post office sells most things." He forced a friendly smile as he spoke, whilst he waved to a browsing holiday maker who left the shop empty-handed. He checked no one else was around, and lowered his voice to a whisper, "I told you never to come here. What are you playing at?" It was all he could do to stop himself from grabbing hold of him and throwing him against the wall.

"Just on my way out of the village, thought I'd stop by and give you the nod." The biker stood firm and glared.

Dan's face reddened. "Go. And don't come back in here again." His eyes darted to and from the doorway, conscious of any locals passing.

"Cheers, I'll get tabs around the corner then, and for the record, you don't give me my orders." The biker smiled, and as he headed out of the door, knocked over a pile of egg boxes, which smashed on the flagstone floor, and immediately seeped yokes. "Oops."

Dan took a deep breath and reluctantly allowed him to leave without any further drama. He couldn't afford anyone to notice his visitor. He licked sweat from his lips, unease gripped his stomach. He shook his head and muttered a string of obscenities as he began to clear up the eggs and re-box the unbroken. That bloke was reckless, he was getting out of hand, and needed reminding.

A glance at the clock confirmed it was almost closing time. He swung the door shut, and bolted it, turning the 'open' sign to 'closed'. At least he could tackle the mounting paperwork over some lunch. Wednesday's half-day closing was his saviour since having to cover the shop. Daisy leaving meant he needed to be in several different places at once, and the pressure felt like a vice, tightening a little more each day. He worried, that soon he wouldn't be able to breathe at all. He had not heard from Daisy since she left for Portugal so abruptly. He had not believed her when she gave him the ultimatum, and every day since, he regretted this.

Colleen liked to brag about their 'business', how she and her husband ran the farm shop and the dairy brand, but the reality was, she did nothing. In fact, she hindered: caused scandal, sullied their reputation, piled more shit into his lap to sort. The one time she 'helped him out' by covering a morning in the shop, it would have been easier to put an ad in the local paper, to apologise to everyone she offended, than deal with all the complaints one by one. Not long after Daisy left, he promised Colleen that she could choose their next shop assistant, but as always, the shop remained low in her priorities, and she had done nothing about it. He sighed, aware that the initial money for the business came from Colleen – that he needed her signature on practically everything.

He could not go on trying to run everything alone, so he pulled open the invoice drawer and grabbed the small card, on which was neatly written: TEMPORARY SHOP ASSISTANT REQUIRED IMMEDIATELY. POLITE. FRIENDLY. RELIABLE. ENQUIRE WITHIN, and swiftly taped it to the door. Colleen would have to get over it, he could not go on any longer, trying to run everything.

Arriving home, Colleen's car had not moved. In what state would he find her today?

"Hey, Col?" He threw his keys in the bowl and headed out to the back of the house, where he could hear the jets on the jacuzzi humming.

"Hey you! good morning at the shop? Are you coming in? I'm naked..."

"Not right now, got too much to sort out, invoices need paying, wages need authorising. You know, the everyday things that keep our finances healthy?" He squeezed his thumbs and exhaled. "You could make us lunch though; I bought some fresh bread home."

"Okay." Her face dropped the suggestive smile. "Give me five more minutes, then I will make food, you want a juice too?" Her enthusiasm evaporated and she leant back and closed her eyes.

Dan nodded, doubtful lunch would appear, and picked up the pile of papers from the basket on the side, as he headed through the utility room into the office. It was easily his favourite room in the house, despite the pressures of work he juggled whilst there. He could lock himself away from the world. A huge window flooded the room with light and afforded him an unspoiled view of the fields beyond their garden, and

11

the Malvern hills in the distance. Sometimes he would stare out towards them, and wish he were at the furthest point he could see, walking on top of the highest hill. Anywhere, but home. It hadn't felt like a home for so long, it was purely somewhere he slept. An address for post. There was nothing homely about the house. It was like living in a furnished rental, soulless. The only room he really liked was his office, and that was because he had bothered to put his own stamp on it over the years, source furnishings and pictures. It was his own space, and Colleen tended to steer clear. He often wondered why they bothered to have such a big house, the amount it cost to run. That simply compounded his sinking mood, each time his key went in the door.

He reached deep into the back of his top drawer, pulled out a mobile and dialled. A familiar click confirmed someone was listening.

 "No one is supposed to come into my shop. You know that. Why the plan change?"

A deep sigh preceded, "We can up the ante whenever we choose Dan. You don't call all the shots, you need us."

"It's too risky. Don't let him come to the shop again. We cannot risk being linked. Don't you want this to work?"

"All you need to do, is keep the money flowing, and leave the rest to me, I have a few ideas to speed things up a little. We have something big on her."

"Like?" Dan scratched his head.

"I told you, leave the detail to us, the least you know the better."

"Something big though?" But the call ended before he got an answer, and Dan switched off the phone, returning it to the hiding place in the back of the drawer. He took a deep breath and clicked his neck both sides.

The bank had called and left an urgent message, for him to contact them. He knew what it would be about but would have to act as though it was all new information. So, he left it for now, it would wait while he got his head straight, and perfected sounding surprised for when they broke the news.

"Would you like some bread with your lunch?" Colleen stood naked, dripping water on his floor. She placed the loaf on his desk and spun him to face her.

Upon his wall, a poster-sized framed picture, in black and white watched the scene. It was of Colleen in her early modelling days, fresh faced in a jean advertising campaign. That was his Col, not this pathetic woman begging for attention. She pushed her breasts towards his face and lifted his hand. "Let's skip lunch, I've a much better idea..."

Dan tore his hand away and stood. "You're dripping water everywhere. I'll make my own."

"What is it with you? You're my husband for Christ's sake!"

Dan turned around. "And?"

"Well, you make me feel like such a whore, for trying to have sex with my own husband."

Dan shrugged and swiped the soggy loaf from his desk. "Cheese or ham?"

SHERRY

Sherry opened the door, hoping a breeze might waft through the stifling shop. The air was, as predicted by the forecasters, unbearable, and even the two fans which Dan had kindly installed were not helping. Her small paper hand fan seemed the only thing capable of creating temporary relief.

The village was busier than usual, bustling with holiday makers stopping by for an ice cream or fresh loaf of bread. The new campsite at Filly Farm, certainly increased their takings and she had already upped her hours. Although she never saw herself working in a shop, she was enjoying this role and chatting to the customers. Her nosy nature absorbed every detail, and she was learning about who was who quickly. It was always useful to know a bit about the locals, who to watch out for, who was related to who. You never knew when that kind of information would come in handy.

The shop felt chic and trendy. She loved the sage green paint and the grey wicker, used all around to display the foods. They had obviously spared no expense on kitting out the place, judging by the quality of the chunky wooden countertop; reclaimed from an old French farmhouse table, according to Dan.

"Morning Joan, the usual?" Joan was their most regular, loyal customer, and it seemed she didn't take kindly to new faces.

"Morning Miss, I am capable of selecting my own items, thank you all the same."

Sherry re-tied her apron, and adjusted the bread shelves, which Dan had already stacked early at delivery.

"No Dan again today?" Joan placed her eggs and milk on the counter and fussed with her head scarf. Why did old people still wear a mac and headscarf in the height of summer?

"Only me I'm afraid." Sherry smiled. "He has a lot on."

"Well, I will have that loaf there. Not that one, *that* one." Joan pointed at the row of identical batons and placed her money on the counter. "Hmm, well there you have it, I credited him with more sense than this."

"Sorry? I don't follow you." Sherry responded and gave Joan her change.

"Taking on another outsider." She packed her items into her worn shopping bag and glared at Sherry. "Barely got used to Daisy, and then she left. Left him in a right pickle and that surprised me, I will tell you. Didn't seem that sort."

Her words trailed behind her as she hobbled out into the blazing sun, beneath her coat. Sherry felt faint thinking about all the layers she wore, and muttered, "Grumpy old bag."

She checked Dan's lists of jobs to do in the diary and settled on pricing up the snacks. Her tummy rumbled and she fought the urge to gobble up a flapjack.

"Put those snacks down…"

Sherry jumped and gasped, "Bloody hell Dan, I wondered who that was…"

"Sorry, came in through the back, to grab some paperwork. I hear Joan is still giving you a tough time then?"

"It would seem so, but it'll be fine, I can handle her." Sherry stared at her boss; she was warming to him. He was not her usual type, but his face lit up on the rare occasions he cracked a smile. Today he was clean shaven, and she preferred him carrying stubble, but he smelt nice and looked after himself. Easy on the eye, with a floppy mop of strawberry hair.

"You still okay for me to be off tomorrow?"

"I guess, anything nice going on?"

"I promised myself a walk, any suggestions?"

"The Malverns?"

"Are they the big hills you can see from here?"

"Yep, used to love roaming those hills, before...before it got so busy here." He stood and scratched his head. His mind was far away from the shop, what was he thinking about? Sherry straightened the shelf which she had begun to date-check and reached into the back to wipe it down.

"Here, take one of these." Dan took a map from the 'local walks' stand. "In case you get lost."

"Thanks." Sherry blushed, took the map and folded it neatly into her apron pocket. He looked dazed. "You okay?"

"Me? Yeh, I'm all good." His voice did not echo the reassuring words. "Right, must get on. You okay here? Call if you want me." He sprung out of the back door to where he had parked.

Sherry followed him out and lingered for a moment in the sunshine. He pulled his sunglasses over his eyes and sped away in his Range Rover, with a wave. He was not a happy man, despite his efforts to convince the world otherwise.

She reflected about her initial enquiry for her job, and how he portrayed his family business, and 'country living' lifestyle, it all felt idyllic. But she had not witnessed the same man, in the weeks since she joined the shop. This man was darker, brooding – seemed to have a permanently furrowed brow, regardless of any smile which may appear beneath. She shrugged. Time would tell.

The shop phone rang, and Sherry sprinted back inside and around the counter to answer it, slightly out of breath. "Morning, Appleyard Store…"

"Is Dan there?"

"No, sorry he's just this moment left…"

"Why did it take so long to answer? We prefer it to be answered within 3 rings. Anyway, who is this?"

"It's Sherry. Can I help?" Anger bubbled within as she inhaled a deep breath.

The line was silent for a moment, as though the caller was thinking what to say next. "Sherry? Are you the new Daisy?"

Sherry puzzled the strange comment. "Well, if you mean the new shop assistant then, yes. As far as I know, Daisy went to Portugal."

"Yes, of course, and you have been there how long Sherry?"

"About three weeks. Sorry, who is this?"

"Colleen, Dan's wife. Funny, he didn't mention you. He knows I like to give our staff the once over…"

"Oh, Hi Colleen, it's lovely to chat to you, I was only taken on temporarily, maybe that's why?" The silent line felt uncomfortable. "Sorry, but I have customers waiting, so…" Sherry glanced around the empty shop, proud of how easily she lied.

"Yes, yes of course, sorry. I must pop by some time Sherry. Show my face. Let you know who your bosses are."

Sherry's stomach lurched inexplicably, and she felt the urge to end the call. "I will be with you in one moment," Sherry called out into the vacant space. "I have a queue now Colleen, I must go before we get complaints."

"Of course, you must, we wouldn't want that. See you soon."

Sherry slammed down the receiver as though it burned her hand. She chewed her lip and sought to untangle the way Colleen had made her feel. Something was off about her. Maybe that phone call went some way in explaining Dan's mood...things not so blissful at home. She gulped water from her bottle and washed her hands in the little sink behind the counter, dousing freezing water over her beetroot face.

It ended up being a steady morning, which flew by and distracted Sherry from dwelling on the mysterious Colleen. In between customers she had the ingenious idea of stock-checking their iced-cream by leaning into a freezer every few minutes. It was almost as good as installing aircon and she deliberately took her time with this job, absorbing every second of ice exposure. She was almost finished, and leaning into the final freezer when a voice commanded her attention.

"Don't leave that freezer open for too long, it will ruin the stock."

Sherry slammed the freezer door and spun around to face a woman, who she knew instantly to be Colleen. She wore a white vest and navy shorts, with wedge sandals. Sunglasses covered most of her freckled face, and her red hair was piled up high on top of her head in a messy bun. She slumped her handbag on top of the counter and put one hand on her hip. She was not smiling as such. It was like the Mona Lisa, open to interpretation. Sherry's mind flashed a fleeting memory.

"Can I help you?" Sherry enquired, as though she were a customer. It was fun messing with people sometimes.

The woman laughed, "Oh! How funny. You don't know who I am, do you? Of course you don't, why would you?"

Sherry's mind sought to recall where she had seen Colleen before, her eyes narrowed: she was the lady arguing with the biker, the day she moved into the cottage. She shifted her weight from leg to leg, fighting the unease which slowly crept across her.

"I'm Colleen, Dan's wife, and *your* boss. We spoke a few hours ago!" Colleen thrust her hand out in greeting and squeezed Sherry's harder than necessary.

Sherry faked a smile and nodded. What was it with this woman? She seemed to evoke intense reactions in her, and her gut instinct was that this lady was to be watched, her vibe was off.

"Still haven't caught up with Dan, so..." Colleen shrugged and glanced around the shop, as she sprayed antibacterial gel onto her hands and rubbed away their handshake. "Oh, be a darling, will you get those front windows cleaned, they are looking rather sad and neglected."

"Mike only came yesterday morning, and I finished dressing that window an hour ago!" She bit her tongue and cursed her reactive answer.

Colleen glared; her lips tightened. She no longer looked like the beautiful woman she first appeared to be. "Well, *Sherry*." Colleen took a step towards her. "I would be most grateful if *you* could give them a clean, they are terribly streaky, perhaps Dan needs to have a word with Mike, because he's not doing a very good job in my book. And I'm sorry to say, but if this,"

Colleen pointed to the window with the arm of her sunglasses, "is AFTER your attempt at window displays, you may want to rethink your position here, because frankly, you're not very good at this, are you?" She fixed a puzzled look on her face, staring, provoking.

Sherry swallowed her own words which threatened to cut Colleen down, and instead forced out a polite monotone response, "Of course, you're right! Now I look at it again, it is lacklustre. I will get right onto it. In this weather, they'll be dry in no time, and I can get some ideas off the internet for the display." Her internalised rage forced a grimacing smile to her face, and she could feel the muscles in her jaw contract.

Colleen swiped her bag, flung it over her shoulder and ran her finger along the shelves, wiping away imaginary dust. "Good girl. I will look forward to visiting again and finding your improvements." She pulled her sunglasses back over her eyes. "Daisy is so missed around here, such a hard worker and her windows were always so on-trend, you know that rural but classy vibe. If you could go for that, I think I would feel so much more comfortable. Oh, and give those shelves an extra polish too, we mustn't let our standards slide. Perhaps if you were to take a look at our Instagram account, you could see some of the previous displays. Might spur you on; give you some ideas, you obviously need inspiring." She sauntered out of the shop with a high, dismissive wave of her hand, oblivious to the fury left in her wake.

Sherry balked at her new boss's treatment. She stomped up and down the shop, with clenched fists. If she didn't need the job so badly, she would never have stood for that. Her silence came from a desperation to stay– she knew she must play the game for now. But that red-haired bitch, was nasty.

DAN

Dan watched from his office window and wondered if Sherry took his advice and went up to the Malverns after all. He used to spend stolen hours up there, breathing in the air, feeling alive. He and Daisy would drive separately, park in different car parks in the beginning, to avoid being discovered. By the end they were less bothered, and in some ways, he hoped someone would 'out them'. But no one did. And then she left him, vowing it was over. And now, left alone with Colleen, he was pretending all was well in public, hiding their sham of a marriage.

He hated her. She was nothing of the woman she pretended to be when they first met: a successful young model, grounded and clean, who earned a small fortune. The early days were fun, and they spent every moment alone, ripping off each other's clothes. But it was all a lie. With the body of a goddess, she kept him involved long after his mind dis-engaged from her. With his carnal urges fed, he could ignore the rest. But as he got older, this was no longer enough, and now, she turned his stomach. The more desperate she got, the further away he drew.

When Daisy first left, he messaged her incessantly and called her mobile, but it always went straight to answer phone. She really meant what she said. It was over. He should have agreed to divorce Colleen, then she would never have stormed away forever.

His mind drew him back to the hills, and Sherry. She was somewhat of a mystery still- and he knew little about her. She rarely gave much away, a closed book. She lacked charisma but was a good worker, and that was exactly what he needed right now. It enabled him to continue chasing new stockists and furthering their brand's reputation, which was required if the company was to move forwards.

He came alive when performing in front of clients, and sometimes he left believing his own lies about his family-run business, which 'he and his wife strive to make successful'. What a joke, he could not even spend more than five minutes in her company, before his face twitched and his fists clenched. Colleen had no idea about business, her mind was consumed with herself, and her own desires.

A shrill laugh set his teeth on edge and marked her arrival home. She was not alone. The gaggle of 'users' whom she considered friends, frequented their home and greedily consumed everything their lifestyle offered. Chinking of champagne-filled glasses began immediately, as did the rumble of jacuzzi jets.   For once, he was glad she was accompanied by the rabble, because it suited his needs, and he could not have planned the scenario better himself.

He silently closed his office door to the noise and opened the email from his bank, reading the words over and over, as though they were new and provoking.   He already played a blinder, when speaking with the bank manager, who revealed the large sums of money which Colleen had been withdrawing, feigning shock and incomprehension. He had asked them to email him the details, so that he could go through the figures with her. Now he looked at the large sums taken out and his heart thumped, as he encouraged his brain to digest the words, the amounts. This was it.

He looked at the stain on his rug, from when Colleen last threw wine at him. He traced his fingers over the scar on his chin, where she smacked him with the hoover, in a rage. He didn't need too much help in psyching himself up, it was even her fault Daisy had left him. That was enough. Daisy was reason enough. He thought about how Colleen drove her away and drew his anger up inside. His fists compressed into tight balls and pounded his desk.

He flew through the utility room, out across the kitchen, into the garden. Discarded clothes scattered the floor, and the jacuzzi roar heightened with the frolicking party occurring within.

"Turn it off!" he screamed.

"Darling, come in, we don't mind do we girls?" Colleen lifted her glass and giggled.

Her pathetic offer further rose his heart rate, and he thought he may have gone too far and could be having a heart attack. His anger was all-consuming, and his chest wound so tight, his face twisted.

"What? What is it?" Colleen stood up, clad only in skimpy bikini bottoms, his face inciting fear. Colour drained from hers by the second.

"Turn this fucking thing off."

Colleen clambered to the control panel, shushing her companions, as the rumbling ceased. All that could be heard was the fizzing of champagne bubbles and Dan's own heavy breaths.

"Leave, all of you...get your shit together and fuck off out of this house!"

Low mumbling surfaced from the women, as they fought to cover themselves on exiting the water.

"What the hell do you think you're doing Dan? What's going on? Girls? I'm so sorry for my husba..."

"Shut the fuck up you idiot. What have you done? Why do I work my nuts off for us, this? What's the fucking point?"

"What is it? What the hell's got into you?"

"You! What have you been doing with all our money?"

29

Colleen climbed out of the jacuzzi and shouted after the fast-moving exodus, "I'll call you later...I'm so sorry about this everyone." She craned her neck to watch the last woman close the door behind them all, as they struggled to dress on the way to the door. "Well, if that wasn't the most embarrassing moment of my life..."

"You... you're a joke. Honestly, is that all you care about? What people think? Those people aren't your friends...they use you for this..." He unclenched his fist and pointed to their property, "for your money, for what they can get out of you. Out of us! Can't you see that? Are you that fucking blind. No, maybe you're desperate for friends and the only way you keep them, is by buying them."

"That's cruel." She wrapped a towel around her body and stood facing him.

"Cruel? I'll tell you what's fucking cruel. Me working myself into an early grave, and you, you're throwing money around like it's worth nothing. You contribute nothing."

"Me?" She flew over to him and jabbed her forefinger into his chest. "You would have none of this if it wasn't for me. When you met me, you were a penniless NOBODY. Now, you are a rich businessman, local hero for your charity contributions. People know your name, because of ME! And you, you haven't even got the decency to talk to me or look at me even for God's sake. What do you want from me? Because I am fucked if I know anymore!" She gasped for breath.

He lowered his voice. "You took half a million pounds from the backup account, why?"

Colleen lifted a glass to her mouth and guzzled it before repouring.

"I'm waiting?"

"Don't talk to me like a child. It's my fucking money Dan, and you are not my keeper. You don't get to make up all the rules. Oh, and I thought you were going to let me do the hiring at the shop, but you can't let me even have that, can you?"

"How long? How long is it since Daisy left? Do you even know? I have been covering since then, I cannot do it all, you fucking moron. I waited and you did NOTHING!" Dan's nostrils flared. He grabbed her neck and the glass smashed to the floor as he pinned her against the wall. "Where is the money?" His low whisper escaped through his clenched teeth.

31

Despite her restricted breath, she remained calm, but her eyes widened, and she licked her lips, suggestively. "It's gone. But on the bright side, this is the closest we've been in some time."

He released her and she dropped to the floor, clasping her neck, and shaking her head. "Forget it Dan, it's long gone..." she called after him as he headed towards the front door. He grabbed his keys from the bowl. "Where are you going now? To fuck your new assistant? She's no Daisy."

Dan stopped at the front door, he wanted to kill her, and if he went back now, and responded to her goading, he might. He took a deep breath and pushed himself through the door, away from his now howling wife. "Dan! Come back! Please Dan! Stay, don't leave me..."

Outside, the bedraggled women awaiting their taxi, huddled in a buzzing group, silenced with his appearance. He stared at them for a moment, fighting the urge to tell them all to fuck off, and sped away in his car. She would push him too far one day, he should have listened to Daisy. On the plus side, he had just given the performance of his life.

SHERRY

Sherry savoured her short walk to work. Beautiful weather accentuated the varying shades of leaves and bright sunshine streamed through the canopy. Often, she would pause and creep along, hoping she may catch sight of a grazing deer, or snuffling boar.

The seductive countryside quickly worked its magic, and she missed nothing from her previous city life. Here she was different and could distract herself with healthy things. In her mind she had drawn a line to the past, that person no longer existed. She hated what the 'old her' had become and was glad to leave that shadow behind. Now was when her life really began. A healthy, wholesome one.

She was surprised when the little cottage was gifted to her in her uncle's will. This stroke of luck proved to be love at first sight, and although it was tiny in proportion, it felt as if it was supposed to belong to her. Fate, or a higher power, was steering her life the right way for once. This brought comfort and she liked the person she saw reflected in the mirror these days, which bore little resemblance to the Sherry of old.

She pushed through the shop door, closed, and locked it behind her. "Hey boss!" Dan turned around and Sherry gasped, "Sorry but you look like shit."

"Cheers, I know."

"Shall I make us drinks? We still have half an hour until we open." Sherry was already putting them together. "Don't worry, I know how you like it."

"Thanks. I must get to the producers today, check in with them, and I could do without it, to be honest."

"You may want to get a fresh shirt Dan; you have a big mark on the back of that one. Here you go, get this down you." She handed him a steaming mug, and gently touched his arm with a warm smile.

"Yeah, need to swing by home on the way."

"Did you know that Colleen came in? I didn't know she wasn't fully in the picture about me working here." She watched his face, as though trying to read his expressions. He didn't give much away, he was thinking about other things, not entirely invested in the conversation.

"Yeah, oh don't worry it's all fine. She likes to keep her hand in, that's all."

Sherry continued to watch Dan over the rim of her mug. He had laughter lines around his eyes and long eyelashes. She decided not to elaborate on the exchange she and Colleen had. It wasn't anything she couldn't handle. She had survived much worse in the past and it would take a lot more than a bitchy conversation to wrong-foot her.

"Thanks for this. Feeling a bit better already. How was your hill walking?"

"Fine, I didn't do the full walk, but spent the morning up there. Nice to feel so free, isn't it? I can see why you recommended it to me. Thanks."

Dan nodded. "There's a lovely pub if you know where to look, does a great Sunday lunch."

"Oh? Perhaps you can give me the details, it sounds perfect." Maybe one day we could go together, she wanted to say.

Dan smiled. "Right, I must get on now. By the way, you're doing a great job and if you are interested, I was thinking you could make it more permanent."

Sherry beamed. It was lovely to be given a compliment, the first in a long time. It felt good.

35

"Did you say you had a reference? It feels like forever ago in one way, since you started, and I cannot remember what we said about it. If I put you on the books, I will need it for the company records, the shop is part of a bigger picture you see." Dan turned to swill his cup in the sink.

"Well…thanks." Sherry fought the stuttering which threatened to steal her words. "Can I think about it, I mean I do enjoy the job, but I didn't plan to work in a shop, that's all." Her cheeks flushed, and she crossed her fingers that he would not read into her answer.

"No worries, but for the record I would be sad to see you go, you've helped me out of a hole. One person can only do so much."

Sherry sipped on her coffee; her eyes followed Dan as he left through the back.

"Call if you need me, as you know I'll be out and about today."

"Okay boss." Tears pricked at her eyes, perhaps her past could not remain buried after all. Maybe she could stall the temporary position for a little longer, Dan may even be her referee for her next job…she must not let this defeat her, it was only another obstacle, that's all.   Anyway, Dan had more than enough on his plate to worry about. Colleen was a handful alone, without the pressures of running his businesses, so with a little luck, he would not follow it up.

A knock at the window stole her attention. It was Joan. "Hold on, I'll open up!"

Joan pointed to her watch. "A minute late opening, I will be telling Dan you know."

Sherry sighed, "Morning Joan, how are you today? Can I help you with anything?"

"No. No need to help me. I can manage and don't bother with your fake niceties, lady."

Sherry wedged open the door and stole a few deep breaths. "Joan, I must have done something to offend you, but cannot work out what it could be. I am polite, and helpful." Sherry touched her arm gently and made her way round to the till.

Joan recoiled, but as Sherry took her place behind the counter, she held Joan's gaze and smiled at the wrinkled grey lady.

Joan said nothing and looked away; her usual bravado seemed to have evaporated into the hot July air. Sherry tilted her head and tried to reconnect with

Joan's eyes, eventually locking them into her stare. "Because you are so hostile with me, and I wondered why? Even Dan has noticed."

The corners of Joan's mouth curled upwards, but not enough to confirm a smile. "Can I have a loaf of bread please and a pint of milk. That's all for today, thank you."

Sherry smiled. "Are you happy for me to choose the bread?"

Joan nodded and shuffled in her purse through the change compartment. "That should be the right money." She popped the loaf and milk into her shopper. "Well Dan notices most things, and we are all entitled to our own thoughts and opinions. Goodbye, and thank you."

"My pleasure Joan, see you tomorrow." She hoped her tone did not reveal the sarcasm in which it was spoken, and as Joan turned away to leave, Sherry's eyes narrowed. She hated being judged by a stranger, being spoken to as though she wasn't good enough. In this new life, she vowed to make sure people respected her, treated her right. But Joan was acting like she knew her from before. Perhaps her uncle had 'put her in the picture?' No, she would not be keeping that to herself. She would have told Dan in a heartbeat.

The shop was in great order, because she had worked hard on it, even staying on longer some days, to finish tasks. She didn't shout about it or expect any extra pay, happy to be able to help Dan out.   Annoyingly, and she would never admit it out loud, but Colleen had been right about the window display, and the new version was a triumph.

She had gone online, as instructed by Colleen and signed up to Instagram. She invented a username, to protect her identity from anyone in her past finding out where she had gone. She wasn't going to actively use it, but it was useful for information gathering.

She found the shop account and scrolled through the posts. Daisy's windows were pretty and stylish, they had opened her mind up to more creative possibilities. It appeared that Daisy had controlled the account before, and there were a couple of pictures of her, behind the counter in her apron, and stood in the doorway. Dan had liked them, but no sign of Colleen, except for the opening day picture of Daisy stood with them, with the hashtag #dreamteam.

Overall, Dan and Colleen were vacant on the web, except for official business information. Colleen had her own Wiki page, but it was out of date, although Sherry had to admit, she was utterly stunning in her modelling days. Dan's Instagram was set to private, so she only had access to his profile picture and that was of the shop.

She glanced around, the only places left to clear behind the counter, were the crammed drawers and over-spilling baskets. The top drawer was mainly full of scissors, pencils and the usual bits and bobs gathered over many years. She pulled out of the bottom drawer a pile of thankyou cards banded together, from appreciative customers. Out of date leaflets went into the bin, and she used the current ones to replenish the 'local attractions' stand.

Underneath, at the very bottom of the drawer, was a notebook. She flicked through the scrawled-on pages, and a photograph fell to the floor. Sherry stooped and picked it up. It was Dan, quite a recent one, as he still wore the same shirt now. He looked happy and his eyes reflected his smile. The young lady, looked adoringly back up at him. She flipped the photograph over, but there was nothing on the back.

Grabbing her phone, she scrolled through and paused on the pictures of Daisy, and compared the photograph next to it. It was definitely Daisy stood with Dan and they appeared intimate, as though a secret, joyous moment had been snapped with a backdrop of the Malverns. No wonder he was so fond of those hills, that must have been where he spent time with Daisy, who clearly, he was having an affair with. Of course, this was only a hunch, but this photo would be dynamite in Colleen's hands. Perhaps she should return the book and the photograph discreetly to Dan, or destroy it? Maybe for now, she could keep hold of it, keep it safe. Something about Colleen was off. She recalled the day in the woods by her cottage and was intrigued to know what that was all about. Her gut reaction was that this photo could cause all sorts of trouble, and she had had enough of that to last two lifetimes.

She tucked the notebook and photograph into her handbag. She hadn't mentioned to Dan about Colleen's argument she witnessed, on her first day in the woods, it was none of her business, for now. She really wanted to keep this job, not only financially but for her own sanity, which surprised her. Besides she felt as though she and Dan, were building something, getting to know each other. Maybe she would tell him if the time was right, but she couldn't bring it up out of the blue.

She seemed to be collecting other people's secrets and it didn't sit well. This was supposed to be a new beginning, less drama, no lies, but she could not help feeling protective of Dan. If Colleen was the bitch Sherry already decided she was, Dan's life must be full of crap, and he didn't need anything else to weigh him down judging by his under-eye bags, which darkened by the day.

DAN

Ironically, despite his desperation, he was on fire in his client meetings, and had more business than he could realistically manage in the pipeline. He would need to get a load of bank staff in the factory, and a temp in the office to help with the admin. It was a dream, his hard work finally coming to fruition and now he wished he had not chosen the path he had, with Colleen. The trouble was, he always knew there would be no going back once he started that, those kinds of people don't back off because you change your mind. He had to see it through, they would make sure of that. He wondered if he could gather enough funds to pay them off, but it wouldn't work, not without it being questioned by the accountants.

 For 15 years he had given his all to the business, everything. He built their reputation from nothing, smoothed the edges when Colleen fucked up, and had contacts in the local papers who would run positive stories and lose the negative scoops. She had no part in any of it. Except she was a signatory, because it was her modelling career which set the initial business up back in the day. It was a joke, her increasingly erratic behaviour meant her signing anything big, depended on her mood. And this was a problem, one that caused him a mother of a headache.

He swung the car into the pub car park and pulled up around the back, so that his car would not be seen from the road. He wanted a bit of peace, not Colleen rocking up and then having to play the 'happy couple' game.

"Bit early for you to be in here Dan, you alright?" Smokey, the landlord poured him a pint.

He downed it and nodded. "Join me? One for yourself?"

"Cheers, I will, not so often I see you these days."

"Don't get a moment. How's business? Picked up since covid?"

Smokey supped his pint, and froth clung to his moustache despite him licking his lips. He nodded, "Good, much busier food wise, and people booking events. A lot of people mentioning your name to be honest Dan, you must recommend us a lot on your travels."

"It's nothing, easy for me to do. Often get asked for places to get good food and ale."

"Well cheers. Much appreciated."

"And you?"

"Oh, you know. One of those days today, thought I might hole up in here for the rest of it, another pint please. I'll sit in the corner by the fireplace."

Smokey shook his head. "Well, here is as good a place as any, but I'll do you a sandwich to wash these pints down, you knocked that first one back a bit quick."

Smokey called out to his wife for the food and wiped down the bar. "You sit, and I will bring it over."

Dan slumped into the armchair, as his phone alerted him to another message from Colleen, it was the fifth in an hour. He turned it off and put it away in his pocket. "Smokey, can you bring me a whiskey with that sandwich, a large one."

Smokey nodded, and Dan ignored the look of concern on his friend's face. He felt like getting bladdered. It was a close-knit village, and he often wondered how much they all knew about Colleen and her 'habits'. They were mainly too polite to say much, but there were whisperings. His eyes and ears were Joan, she always spoke her mind, and if anything reached her, she was never afraid to ask him directly. He wouldn't always give an honest answer, his priority was to protect the business, but he appreciated her frankness.

Jackie brought out a doorstep sandwich, garnished with salad. "Here Dan. Hey! Haven't seen you in here for a long time, how's Col?"

Dan stared at Jackie, before answering, "Colleen is…" Unsure how to answer he took a large bite of the sandwich. He pointed to the plate and with a full mouth, nodded appreciatively.

"Good, it's on the house. All those deals you have been good enough to push our way. About time we showed appreciation."

Jackie stood, and turned away, but before she took a step, she leaned in. "I hope everything is okay, I know you work hard, and I know it's not always, well, things aren't always easy for you. But if you ever need a friendly face, then please come here because we think the world of you." She pecked him on the cheek and squeezed his shoulder. Dan smiled. They were a genuine couple, and popular with everyone. Judging by her concern, the gossips from the 'jacuzzi incident' were already polluting the rumour mill. That was something; and quicker than he imagined too.

He necked his whisky and cradled his pint, watching a rowdy group of young farmers arrive and order late lunches. He was playing the injured party role well, but how many times had he left functions early, spiriting Colleen away and hoping no one noticed her inappropriate flirting or slurring nonsensical conversations. Now, he needed them all to notice, and to see him as a wounded bird. He wanted them to say, "poor Dan, the mans a saint, how does he put up with her?" He wanted them all to feel that way.

He drained the last of his pint and secured the money beneath his plate. He would pay his own way, never be in debt to others, was what he learned from his father. How many times had he cursed himself for not remembering that when it came to Colleen?

Smokey was too busy pulling pints to notice him sneak out the door. For a moment he fiddled with his keys, it wasn't far to drive home, and he didn't feel drunk...but he pushed them into his pocket and headed up the road, towards home. Last thing he needed was a drink-driving ban.

"Hey! Dan?"

He stopped and spun around; it was Sherry.

"Aren't you supposed to be at the shop?"

Sherry caught up and faced him. "Well, I have been, actually I stayed later and cleaned out the fridges, but it's Wednesday – half day closing?"

"Shit, I seem to have lost a day somewhere." He scratched his head and shrugged his shoulders.

"I was going to ask, what you are doing, do you need a black coffee? Perhaps I could give you a lift home? I'm only around the corner and it's no bother."

"What gave me away?"

"I can smell the whiskey. Come on, I have some of our finest coffee beans."

Dan walked along side Sherry in silence, his dark thoughts swirling around his mind. He must be guarded with his words. Sherry was intuitive and seemed to hang on his every word.

"Here we are, told you it wasn't far, come on in. It's lovely to have a visitor to be honest. You are my first!"

Dan followed Sherry in through the front door. It was the tiniest cottage in the village, the former occupant having passed away the previous October. He was friendly with Joan. "I didn't know this was where you lived, Des was one of Joan's friends. Thick as thieves they were."

"Oh, I didn't know that. Hadn't seen Uncle Des since I was little. He left me this cottage in his will, caused all sorts of family chaos, because no one understood why. He had fallen out with everyone, and my brother said he only left it to me to cause 'bad feeling' in death, like a final hurrah."

Dan watched as Sherry ground the coffee beans, and his nose appreciated their aroma. He lent against the back kitchen window, where a tiny window seat had been created with a patchwork cushion. It was the smallest kitchen he had ever seen, but cosy and somehow seemed to have everything you could need.

"I was so grateful when I found out, I mean, it was a new beginning coming here, an opportunity to start over."

"You must back onto the woods here, in fact I could cut through the back there, walk home that way, save you giving me a lift." The last thing he needed was Colleen accusing him again of shacking up with Sherry. Rocking up in her car, would set her off, besides, he hadn't walked that way for years, it would be cathartic.

"You sure? I don't really know my way around too well yet, but if you know where you are going, that's fine. Now here, drink this."

"Cheers." He accepted the expresso gratefully and stifled a smile. The tiny cups always made him feel like a giant.

"I know you aren't ok, but is there anything, I mean, if you need to talk, I am happy to listen…"

Dan did not want to start involving anyone else, that would complicate everything. "Really, everything is good. This is excellent coffee, but hey, you got it from the best place for miles around." It was a lame attempt at a joke, but he didn't want to get into anything. He finished his drink and put the cup next to the sink. "So, fresh start, eh? Did leaving help? I mean, do you have regrets, and do you mind me asking what you left behind?"

Sherry stood still, startled by his question, her eyes wide. He wondered what nerve he had hit, and the atmosphere suddenly felt awkward. "It's fine, I'm sorry for prying. You don't have to tell me anything. Really. Thanks for the this, you were right, I did need it…now lead me out to that back gate of yours, so I can find my way home." He squeezed her arm and smiled, but he wanted to escape, the house suddenly felt as though it was closing in on him and he fought the urge to run.

"This way." Sherry flicked her head towards the back door and opened it wide. "Follow this path through the garden, and out of the gate."

He waved before sprinting away from Sherry, who he knew was watching him disappear through the trees.

SHERRY

The early morning birdsong had become Sherry's countryside alarm clock. She would have warned against approaching before ten, in her old life, but here, she loved to saunter downstairs, grab an early cuppa and sit on the tatty bench by the lavender. Dan asking her about her previous life the week before, had stirred up feelings and she tried hard to push down the anxiety which they induced. If anyone found out about what happened, she would have to move on, and that was too high a price to pay. This was the first time she felt truly at home and settled. She could almost feel the roots sprouting from her feet into the soil. It would take something huge to tear her away from there. She felt normal, and well balanced, despite ditching her medication. There didn't seem to be such a need for it now. It was as though all of this was her therapy. The outdoors, the trees, the sweet smell of pine.

Luckily, whatever was occupying Dan's mind, and appearing to carve new worry lines daily, was keeping the reference question at bay. He seemed grateful to have someone he trusted watching the shop so that he could flit about where he was needed. There had been no more visits from Colleen, but somehow it felt as though she could appear at any time. She was like a storm brewing or tornado approaching.

Sherry checked her watch, it was only seven, she had an hour before she needed to get ready for work. Her garden needed weeding, but it was blooming with flowers, and one whole border blossomed with beautiful white daisies, stretching up towards the sun. She smiled and felt blessed, but in an instant her mind jumped to the photograph she had found, it was one of those nagging feelings, which you have no reason to feel but she knew she needed to give the picture back to Dan. Were they having an affair, did Colleen find out? Was that why Daisy left? Suddenly her mind swam with questions and possibilities. It may contribute to why Dan's mood seemed so low – he was missing Daisy? Should she give the photograph to him? Although she was not yet ready to confess to witnessing the woodland incident with Colleen, she could at least release herself of one secret if she did.

She texted Dan: **ARE YOU COMING INTO THE SHOP TODAY**? Before she could change her mind.

Dan's reply was instant: **PLEASE TELL ME YOU ARE NOT OFF SICK?**

Sherry: **NO, COULD DO WITH A WORD, SO IF YOU CAN CALL IN – NOTHING URGENT THO**

Sherry drained the last of her cup, expecting a further speedy reply. There was none. She sighed, hoping he wasn't going to think it was to do with her job, and start digging around her past again. She shook her head and silently berated herself, she could have stirred up her own shit now, in trying to help. She washed up her cup on the way to the bathroom, when a bang on her front door made her jump. Who was that at this time of day? She peeped through the window of kitchen and saw Dan's car parked on the road.

"I said it wasn't urgent! I meant you to call into the shop at some point, not rush here now!" Sherry closed the door behind him, ushering him through the tiny hallway into her lounge, where Dan sat on the armchair by the fire. "I wish I had waited now; I didn't think you would be this concerned." But secretly, she

53

loved that he rushed over, and she got an extra few minutes in his company.

"It's not like you to message this early, so it must be something...tell me you're not leaving? Jeez Sherry, that's all I need now, if you knew how much shit I'm dealing with..."

"Woah! You're jumping ahead, no that's not it."

Dan leaned back in the chair. He looked as though he hadn't slept. "Thank God. I think that would have finished me off."

"Well, it's a bit awkward really, it's ...hold on." Sherry disappeared upstairs and grabbed the notebook from next to the printer. She took a deep breath and held it out in front of her. No turning back now.

Dan's eyes narrowed. "What's that?"

"Well, I thought you better have it, because of this..." She handed it over with the photograph. "I thought, that if I could stumble across this, then, well, what if Colleen found it?"

Dan's wide eyes stared at the image, and he swallowed hard. "It's my sister? No, she's, my friend? How about a friendly customer? I could lie, but to be honest, I haven't the energy, do you know who this is?"

"Yes, it's Daisy."

He nodded. "Yep."

"Were you and Daisy…"

"Yep, we very much were." Dan interrupted before Sherry could verbalise what he and Daisy were 'doing'. "How did you know it was Daisy in the picture?"

"Colleen told me to look at the Instagram page for the shop, to get some ideas for the window display. So, I saw her on there."

"Did she? She has got a nerve telling you to do that."

"Is that why Daisy left? Did Colleen find out?"

"Colleen had suspicions, but as far as I know she never knew 100%. Daisy wanted me to divorce Colleen, start a new life in Portugal. But I said no, I didn't want to lose everything I had built up here, how wrong can you be? Money is nothing really when it comes down to it."

"I won't say anything to anyone, I promise. All I wanted was to give this back to you."

"Really appreciate it, your support."

Sherry blushed. "Can't you reach out to Daisy? Track her down?"

"I don't have any information about where in Portugal she went...and I have left messages and sent texts. She doesn't want me anymore. Even her socials have gone quiet- totally off-radar. She really doesn't want me to find her."

"I'm so sorry."

"Whatever Colleen said to her, made her cut me off. I wouldn't be surprised if she told something seriously bad about me... it makes my blood boil." Dan stood and headed towards the front door. "I'm sorry, barging in like this early morning, how self-centred. I'll go open- up. I was on my way anyway – bread delivery...You come in a bit later, say 10? Have a nice soak in the bath or something. From my experience, women come out of bubble baths in a much better state that when they enter it..." He shook his head. "I just realised how patronising that sounded."

"Thanks, I know you're being kind. But the thing is, I only have a shower..."

Dan laughed, and his eyes sparkled. His face relaxed long enough for his permanent creases to disappear, and Sherry smiled.

"In that case, I have no further ideas, but seriously, come in for ten. Thanks for this." He slipped the photograph into his pocket and threw the notebook into the bin on his way out to the front door.

"See you later." Sherry shut the door and headed back to the kitchen for another drink and slice of toast, her head spun. She couldn't imagine Colleen taking that news well, if she ever found out. Weirdly, considering she discovered her boss was cheating, Sherry felt sorry for *him*, not the 'wronged' wife. Something about Colleen was disturbing, and she shuddered. Poor Dan, he honestly looked defeated, beaten down. As she passed the bin, the discarded notebook caught her eye, and she fished it out, carrying it upstairs to her cupboard. She placed it next to the card which advertised her job, the map Dan gave her of the Malverns, and the photo-copied picture of Dan and Daisy, which she had cropped her out of.

DAN

Dan's stomach groaned at the waft of bacon permeating from the kitchen. He headed towards the promise of food, sat at the breakfast bar and poured an orange juice from the jug.

"They say the way to reach a man is through his stomach...I've got bacon on the go, mushrooms, tomatoes, you want an egg too?" Colleen bustled around the kitchen, as though she were housewife of the year. Her humming was irritatingly chirpy.

"You having one?" Dan yawned and stretched.

Colleen paused and her shoulders hunched. "Does it matter? Do you want one or not? It's a simple question Daniel." She froze as she awaited his response.

"No." Dan cleared his throat, "no thanks." He reached across and pulled the daily paper towards him, pretending to scan the page, already wishing he had ignored his hunger and stayed clear of the kitchen until she was done. He silently berated himself, for not knowing better and braced for the inevitable.

"How can making breakfast be so fucking awkward for us? It's literally supposed to be a simple meal, to kick off the day. And yet we still manage to make it so difficult. It baffles me. You baffle me."

Dan sipped his juice, forcing back the words he wished he could scream out.

"I mean," Colleen turned away from the abandoned eggs which continued to sizzle in the pan, "you don't sleep with me, so why bother eating together? Is that how it works darling husband? Because there's no one here, nobody to pretend in front of now." She leant against the work top. "Although after your recent outburst in front of the girls, MY FRIENDS, it appears we have gone way beyond any fucking pretence."

"Sorry did you say, your *friends*? That's a joke, because not one of them hung about to make sure you were ok. They soon scurried away and left you. And let's not forget, that I had just found out you stole half a million pounds. And I know there has been more than that too. Did you think I would wave it off, as though it were nothing? In business, money must be accounted for, but then you wouldn't know anything about that. You're only interested in yourself." He knew he was poking the viper's nest, but he couldn't help it. Hopefully this would be another inch closer to the edge for her.

Colleen slowly sauntered towards him and leaned in close, her negligée spaghetti strap slid down her arm and revealed her breast, she didn't adjust it. "Firstly, you can't steal your own money, honey. It's mine anyway." Her hand was on his shoulder, and he flinched as she spoke into his ear. "Secondly, at least I have friends Dan. And finally, why would I be involved in business, who has a dog and barks?" She spun his stool around to face her, and pushed herself between his legs, wrapping her arms around his neck. "Why can't you loosen up and go with the flow a little. You're always so uptight." Her voice was low, and her finger trailed his jaw.

He recoiled, stood and shoved her away. "Why did you need cash? Why take it out in separate transactions? It doesn't add up, and I don't want our business involved with crooks. I fought hard for my reputation after your drug habits made the news." His voice escalated into an aggressive shout.

"Why does it always come back to that? Have you never done wrong in your life? Are you going to make me pay for that forever? Haven't I paid enough?"

"Enough? You?" Dan's voice rose. "Rehab and spa retreats, whilst I spent every spare moment fundraising and building back our reputation...running myself into the ground!" His hands gripped clumps of his hair, and then he rhythmically pounded his forehead with his palms.

"Oh, I paid, every time your attention wandered. Like a stab to my chest." She followed him around the breakfast bar, blocking his exit from the kitchen with her arms stretched out.

"Whenever you come near me, I feel sick. I can't even bear looking at you, let alone touching you." Dan stared directly into her face, and his lips curled, suppressing a cruel smile. "Imagine being married to someone who turns your stomach, that the thought of fucking them, makes a tiny bit of bile creep up into the back of your throat."

Colleen's eyes filled with tears, and her mouth opened and closed, before she screamed, "You fucking prick, do you know how many offers I get, and turn down because of you? How dare you say these things. You were a nobody Dan, and YOU STILL FUCKING ARE, no balls, no courage."

Dan's fists clenched tight with anger, he needed to get away from her, but he couldn't shut his mouth up. "I heard you were anybody's for a bag of coke, sometimes even just a line."

The glass jug smashed in two, with the blow to his head. He reeled. "You've lost your fucking mind!" His fingers sought the deep welt in his cheek. Orange juice and blood seeped into his white T-shirt. She pounded his back, as he turned away and scowled with pain. "Now you've gone too far, look at me!"

Colleen stopped and her hand flew to her mouth. She reached out to touch his face. "Oh Christ, let me clean that, Dan I'm so sorry."

"Don't fucking touch me, get away!" He reached for the kitchen towel and dabbed at his face, wincing. Silently he acknowledged, that this was the end, no business, money or reputation was worth putting up with this.

Colleen unzipped the first aid kit. "There's some butterfly stitches in here, best use them, let's clean it up first though."

"For fucks sake, leave me alone, will you? I don't want you near me. Why don't you understand that? Get that into your stupid addled brain."

He snatched the case and headed upstairs to the safety of his room. His heart pounded as he peeled away the kitchen towel and checked the wound, it was deep enough but wouldn't require a casualty visit. He locked his door, not in fear, but he could no longer be responsible for his actions were she to come close.

A quiet knock on the door quickly escalated to a pounding. "Please let me in! I need to make sure you're ok! Dan, please! I'm sorry!"

Dan ignored her and flushed away the bloodied kitchen towel. He threw his stained T-shirt into the bin as her whining increased with his silence.

"Is this about her?" She wailed.

Dan stood still, who did she mean? Sherry? He resisted the urge to respond.

"Well, is it? I know you loved her; you've never been affectionate or tender with me."

"Sherry and I are colleagues, nothing more. You're crazy to think otherwise." He must have been seen going into her cottage.

"You know exactly who I'm talking about. Stop playing games. Plain old Sherry, she's no threat. But Daisy, well that was a smack in the face...you couldn't hide that from me."

Dan opened the door and Colleen crumpled into a heap against the banister. Her red eyes stared up accusingly as she hugged her legs tight.

"I'm not playing games, I haven't the energy."

"Daisy, you're in love with her."

Dan leant backwards, what a fucked-up mess. "She's gone now anyway."

Colleen sobbed, "You never looked at me the way I saw you look at her. Why couldn't you love me?"

"I'm sorry. I didn't set out to start anything, but it happened. It's over now though, she's gone, and I can't get hold of her."

"Does that mean I stand a chance again? Could you love me again, now Daisy's gone?" She jumped to her feet and threw her hands together. "Please say it. Say we can try? Please Dan?"

Dan coughed. Shock stole his voice. She really thought they could salvage something from their mess. Was she that deluded? Dan slowly shook his head. "I'm sorry, but you must know it. For me, there's been nothing here for a long time, that's why I could turn a blind eye to your 'extras.'"

"None of them meant anything to me. It was always you Dan. I've never stopped hoping we can turn back the clock, to those days when you couldn't keep your hands off me. Do you remember them? They were good days, weren't they?"

Dan swallowed the lump in his throat. "That was a long time ago, we were both kids."

Colleen clawed at his chest. "Forgive me, for today? Please say you can. And those other men, they were nothing. I did it all for you, to make you feel. To make you jealous."

Dan sighed. His body ached, and he longed to rest. He wanted peace. For all this to be over. "You know me, good at moving on, forgiving."

Colleen's sad smile summed up their marriage- smoke and mirrors. Keeping up appearances for the business' sake. Maybe it was time, to stop the pretence and for them both to have a chance of being happy. But his cheek stung, and he could not muster the energy to begin this conversation, not today. At least the ground was prepared, and he had been honest about there being no going back.

"Friends, at least, please?"

Dan nodded in defeat and patted her back. He had no intention of being anything to her, at least nothing that resembled a friendship.

"I'm sorry about Daisy, really sorry." Colleen sniffed, turned and sashayed into her bedroom, closing the door behind her.

"Yeh, me too," Dan replied, as he switched his phone into camera selfie mode. He pushed his head forward and angled his latest injury. Once satisfied with the picture, he saved it in the folder named 'injuries', alongside the other photographs. He had a feeling that these would be of use, very soon.

SHERRY

"Jeez boss, what happened to you? Have you been in a fight?"

"This? It's nothing." He shrugged. "A drunken stagger into a shed window, its fine."

"Oh. Ok." Sherry hoped her answer sounded more convincing than it felt.

"Everything ok here?"

"Yeh, but Joan hasn't been in for two days…"

Dan's eyes narrowed. "That's unusual, I'll take her some milk and bread round, check in on her. Was she ok, when you saw her last?"

Sherry chewed her lip. "You know Joan, gets a bee in her bonnet sometimes. Who knows?"

Sherry wondered if her blatant confrontation was to blame for the latest boycott of the shop. "Apart from that, it's all fine. Any joy getting hold of Daisy?"

Suddenly aware that she had crossed her fingers in her apron pocket, she acknowledged that she hoped he hadn't managed to contact her. She liked it how things were, Daisy returning would complicate it all. Even if she didn't want her old job back, Dan would be preoccupied and unavailable for her on any level.

Dan shook his head.

"Well, don't give up. She will relent eventually, I'm sure." I hope not, I hope not; her silent thoughts repeated over and over.

"And you? Anyone special around?"

Sherry's stomach flipped. "Me? Nope. Happy bumbling along, doing my own thing, for now at least. I think relationships can sometimes offer more misery than joy. So, I'm working on finding my own happy place before I allow someone else to affect it."

Dan scratched his head. "Sounds sensible enough to me. Right, I'm gone. Off to sign paperwork for the yoghurt distribution but will call and see Joan on the way."

"Here, take her this, they are her new favourites." Sherry wrapped a flaky almond croissant in a paper bag and thrust it into Dan's waving hand. "Don't worry, I will pay for it. Better not tell her it's from me, or she might throw it away."

Dan laughed. Sherry waved him off and took a water bottle from the staff fridge. His injury was no drunken stumble, that was inflicted, and she knew by whom. He seemed to be spiralling downwards, and she remembered how that felt, not so long ago, that was how her life looked. She would have his back from now on, she could look out for him.

She sipped her water; thank God the air was cooler, and she could walk about the shop again without breaking into a sweat. The bell swung her head towards the opening door, and she almost choked. It was the biker man, from her first day in the village. Her stomach lurched with the thought that he would recognise her, had somehow seen her through the fence. But unless he had x-ray vision, she knew this was impossible. Still, she shivered.

"Can I help you?" She sounded much calmer than she felt.

"You sell fags yet?"

"No, but the shop around the corner does."

"Yeh, I know. No boss in today? I'll just take this then." He threw down a flapjack and grabbed a coke from the fridge.

"No, he rarely works in here now. Can I pass a message on for you? You local? I haven't seen you before."

His eyes narrowed. "You ask a lot of questions. No, I'll catch him another day. How much?"

"£4.50 please."

"Bloody hell, what's in the flapjack? Gold dust? Here."
He squeezed into his leather trouser pocket and
pulled out some coins, thrusting them into her hand.

"Thanks, that's spot on." she dropped the warm
money into the till and tried not to think about where
the coins had been festering.

As he left, she washed her hands in the sink and
wondered if he was paying Colleen a visit. Maybe she
was his only connection in the village, but why was he
asking for Dan? Was he a friend of theirs? Maybe
Colleen was having an affair with him, that's what the
argument was about... Her mind reeled with
possibilities. She picked up the phone to call Dan, but
something stopped her. She needed to think things
through more. Why, she had no idea. It felt as
though she were becoming ensnared within a web,
and that the more snippets came her way, the less
chance she had of escape. She didn't like it; this was
supposed to be a fresh start, and yet a smile crept
across her lips and her heart pounded. Something
strange was simmering.

A slow afternoon meant time for overthinking. This
was not ideal; it was an enemy of hers from before.

That was when things usually escalated, when her mind cranked up a gear and imagined all sorts of things were going on. This time, it wandered to her conversation with Dan about Joan, and how she was great friends with Uncle Des. Perhaps that explained the frosty reception, she had received from Joan, maybe she knew about her past? This wasn't the first time the thought has occurred to her, but surely, Joan would not have held onto that, would have taken pleasure in telling Dan all about it? Joan wasn't the type to sit on information as potentially inflammatory as her past. She would have stopped Dan employing her from day one.

Yet the panic still grew and tightened her stomach into a twisting knot. Her breath quickened, Dan was off to see her today, check on her. Why hadn't she come to this conclusion sooner? What if she spilled the beans? Her hands shook and her new reality felt hazy, temporary, as though she was now on borrowed time, awaiting a knock at the door. She would be the village weirdo, and people would cross over to avoid eye contact. Her thoughts sped along like an out-of-control train as she fought to slow her breathing and her smile evaporated.

"Excuse me?"

The voice jolted Sherry back to the reality of the shop, and the enquiring customer stood in front of her.

"You ok? You look as white as a sheet?"

Sherry forced a smile. "Oh, I'm fine. I'm so sorry I didn't see you come in, must be due my coffee and cake!"

"As long as you're ok. Could you tell me if you sell goat's cheese?"

Sherry wiped her sweaty palms on her apron and wandered around the counter. "We certainly do, it's right around here."

Around three, after a couple of hours of solid racing thoughts, the shop phone rang. "Good afternoon, Appleby Stores," her voice answered shakily.

"Sherry, it's Dan, can you hang around at closing time, I need to have a word."

"Oh. Is everything ok?" Sherry felt the room spin a little, and her stomach lurched. He knew.

"I need to speak to you, that's all. I should be back in time for closing, see you then."

He was already gone before she could answer, and her shaking hands put down the receiver. Her mind spun. What would she do? If he knew, it would only be a matter of time before the entire village did too. She couldn't cope with going back to the life she left behind.

Before, after 'it' all happened, she would not leave the house unless there was no one else around. And she would drive miles, simply to go shopping, somewhere she could remain anonymous. That was not an option here, no one was anonymous, and she loved her life now- the thought of losing it all was too much to bear.

Her teeth gnawed at her nails, as she fought the rising panic. This could be the last time she was in the shop before the slander and disgust began? Maybe she should close the shop and go home, she could pretend she was sick. Yes. That's exactly what she would do. She wasn't even pretending, because she felt as though she could throw up at any minute.

She hastily removed her apron, and stuffed it into her handbag, switching off the lights and bolting the door. After securing the till drawer in the safe, she headed out the back door. Her fumbling fingers dropped the keys as she attempted to lock up, desperate to avoid

Dan arriving back, and she hurried along the back lane as fast as she could.

Once the front door closed behind her and in the safety of her own home, embarrassment flushed her cheeks. Fear of her over-reaction inched across her calmer thoughts. It could have been anything he needed to discuss with her, business, Daisy... She cursed her stupidity and took out her phone:

SO SORRY DAN, FEELING SO ILL HAVE HAD TO CLOSE UP AND GO HOME. WILL MESSAGE YOU LATER WITH AN UPDATE.

Now she would have to feign sickness, to avoid looking like a complete lunatic. She carried her phone upstairs and slumped onto her bed, perhaps she would never escape her past. It may hide for a while, but it followed her around like her shadow. Or worse, what if it was still in her, lying dormant, and would be wherever she went.

He hadn't texted back yet, maybe he was driving. Or perhaps he was on his way around to her, to confront her? She would not answer if he did, she was sick after all, and wouldn't answer the door, that was the truth anyway. After a few minutes, her phone alerted her to a text:

SORRY YOU ARENT WELL. WE CAN CATCH UP WHEN YOU'RE BETTER? KEEP ME POSTED. DAN

Her breathing slowed, and the rational thoughts returned. If he knew, he wouldn't want to wait to confront her, he would insist on addressing it. She turned her anger inwards and berated herself for the foolishness of her reactions. If she was going to keep her new life, there was work to be done on her responses.

DAN

When he finally arrived home, Dan was exhausted. He felt as though he was coming down with a lurgy too, perhaps Sherry had passed something on to him. Thank goodness she had texted and was due back in the shop tomorrow. When Daisy was still around, he loved finding excuses to spend time there; steal kisses in the quiet moments. They worked well together, and he felt like a team with her. He and Colleen were never compatible like that. Now it was simply a shop, and it felt empty without her.

He winced at the thought that Colleen had known all along and wondered how often they had been spotted by her, sneaking affectionate glances or gestures. It made him shiver. Daisy had no idea the depths of Colleen's depravity. He had hidden it from her, like a dirty secret. He felt it may sully how she viewed him, if she knew what he was married to. He didn't want Daisy to think anything negative about him. Although, that didn't help his cause, because she left him anyway.

Maybe he was strung out with everything that was going on, it was getting to him. "Hello?" He called out and felt relieved that no answer came back. The hot tub suddenly felt appealing, perhaps he should climb in and relax. He never got to use it much, as Colleen seemed to monopolise it and he would not risk getting in with her. She always read more into it, and he would have to knock her back...it was never worth the argument.

He wearily wandered towards the bench and peeled off his clothes. He switched it on and grabbed a beer from the fridge. As he climbed in and allowed the jets to pound his tense shoulders, he realised how tightly he was wound. He was likely to snap if he didn't try and relax a little.

He still had things to do, for his plan to work, and needed to remain in control to complete it. With a long deep breath, he stared out over the garden, down to the copse at the bottom. It was a moment of sadness, that all of this belonged to him, and he was seldom able to enjoy a moment's peace there. That his home, felt more like somewhere he dreaded to go to, rather than a place to kick back and relax.

He guzzled his cold beer and his thoughts returned to Daisy. Where was she? Did she think about him? He hadn't tried to call her for a while now, accepting that she really was out of his life and no number of texts or calls could change that. The best he could hope for now, was that Colleen would soon crack under the pressure of the blackmail and end up messy. He would be ready this time, he would get everything signed over to him, prove she was not stable enough for the decision making. But, then what? Without Daisy, it all seemed pointless. Her youth and enthusiasm were contagious, and around her, he felt like he could do anything. She believed in him.

The resident peacock strutted along the path, calling for attention, and Dan's eyes narrowed as he realised the garden was looking shoddy. He couldn't remember the last time he had seen their gardener.

He muttered, "For fucks sake, probably another person Colleen has managed to piss off." He made a mental note to call him, to get him back in, before the grounds got too much of a mess. A bottle of something nice and a hefty tip usually tempted people back.

He yawned and pushed the thoughts out of his mind. Draining his beer, he placed the bottle on the side. It felt good to chill out and the only thing which could have improved that moment, was Daisy, in her skimpy bikini. Her hair loose around her shoulders, and her cheeky smile promising some serious action. With her though, apart from the sex, he felt the deepest connection he ever felt with anyone. When he was with her, it felt as though they were supposed to be together.

He drifted off with the hum of the jets, and awoke as Colleen loomed over him, naked. "Hey sleepy head, wake up. It's not a good idea to fall asleep in here, you could drown."

Dan sat upright, a little dazed, still half asleep.

"So, come to think of it, I've just saved your life." She knelt, and her silicone breasts floated up on the water. Repulsion surged through Dan's veins, and he stood up to leave. But Colleen was too quick, and before he could move, she pushed him deep into her mouth. Dan groaned, as Colleen expertly climaxed him. She swallowed, and gently wiped her lips with her fingertips. "I still know what you like, it's not all bad."

Dan climbed out of the hot tub, enraged by his weakness in the moment, disgusted at the thought of her lips around him. This was why he never willingly put himself in these positions with her. It was these moments which provoked false reality. Colleen was not a rational thinking person, her brain was addled by the years of drug abuse. This was something she would cling to and derive hope from. It was only a bodily function, but to her it was power, reassurance that she could still pleasure him. The truth was, it could have been anyone at that sleepy moment, only he was stupid enough not to push her away.

"It's okay Dan, no thanks needed. It was my pleasure." Colleen followed close behind him dripping pools of water all over the floor. "It's not like you to wait for me in the hot tub!"

Dan sprinted up the stairs, closed and locked his bedroom door. He waited for her footsteps to head away before taking a hot shower.

As he threw on some sweatpants and a t-shirt, his stomach groaned. He needed some food. Music blasted from the kitchen, where Colleen stood drinking a glass of champagne. "Want one?"

Dan shook his head, aggravated that she was still naked, and the kitchen was peppered with pools of water. "No, I need food. Can't you use a towel? There's water everywhere." He turned the music off, his head pounded.

Colleen sidled up to him and rubbed his arm. "It's only a little water darling. Now, let me rustle something up for you..."

"No, I'm fine, I can make something." He shrugged her away and rummaged through the fridge. It was a good job they owned a food store, because if it was left to Colleen, the fridge would contain champagne and nothing else. He pulled out some hummus, olives and ham, and plated it up with some fresh bread.

"You are a man of few words..." she slurred.

"It's the best way sometimes." He didn't look up, but busied himself with his food prep.

"Were you like that with *her*?"

Dan ignored her, she was trying to provoke him.

"Daisy, I mean. What were you like with her? I mean, I saw you, many times, holding hands, sneaking kisses when you thought you were alone…but I wonder, was she good in bed? Was Daisy a go-er? Is that why you liked her so, so much?"

Dan's scarlet cheeks puffed. "I didn't like her Colleen, I loved her." He swung to face her, staring into her cold eyes. "And I still do. Not that you know what love means or feels like. If she walked through that door now, I would be gone."

"Poor Daisy. Poor, poor, Daisy. Had no idea what she was getting involved with, did she? I mean, where is she now Dan?" Colleen began frantically opening cupboard doors and lifting objects up, "Daisy are you there? Daisy? Where are you? Poor Daniel, lost his Daisy."

"Shut the fuck up. You're fucking mad. You should know, though, I NEVER felt a fraction of how I feel about her, for you. You were just a good lay, with lots of money. Nothing better for an ego than to say you're dating a rich model. That's all you were to me, an ego boost. Now, well now, you're nothing to me."

The room silenced. A cold eery pause.

"Actually, that's not true." Dan smiled, as he watched hope appear in Colleen's eyes. "You are an utter drain on me, you are a weight around my neck, you are acidic, vile and volatile. And you know nothing about Daisy."

Colleen's hope dissipated, and her cheeks flushed. She slowly turned towards him and one slow step at a time, edged closer. Dan's skin prickled. And his heart pounded. He knew he had ignited her anger.

"No. *You,* know nothing," she spoke almost in a whisper, and he felt her breath on his face.

Suddenly her hands grappled at his neck and torso, her fingernails sliced through his flesh, but his quick reactions gripped her wrists, and he stretched her arms high above her head until her face grimaced in pain.

"WHAT DO YOU KNOW?"

Colleen gritted her teeth. "I wouldn't tell you, even if you choked it out of me."

Flooded with rage, Dan threw her into the wall and flung himself at her, tightening his fingers around her neck. "Well, let's see, shall we?" He spat the words at her, and her eyes widened as his grip intensified.

A cold chill on his neck cleared the mist, he let go of her, and staggered backwards. She writhed in a heap on the floor. "You weak bastard, you can't even do that right, can you?"

Dan pressed his palms against the cool wall and fought to control his breath. "This is bad. Someone is going to end up really hurt."

"You talk as if it hasn't already happened... hurt? You hurt me every day. I don't care about the physical stuff...I know you *feel something* when your anger appears. It's the little things, the lack of interest, the things you don't notice, that are slowly killing me."

Dan shook his head, disgusted with how low they had both sunk.

"She'll never come back to you; you know that don't you? You may finally understand some of the pain I feel...when you accept that."

"If you have ever loved me, if there is anything left, please, do you know where Daisy is?" Dan's eyes implored.

Colleen inched her way along the floor towards Dan, knelt by his legs and pulled him to the ground. "I have always loved you. I love you too much. That's why I stay. Day after day. Because I hope that we can one day be happy again."

Dan sighed and looked away in desperation, dumbfounded that her delusions stretched this far. "What do you know?"

"Have the decency to look at me for Christs sake." She pulled his face back to hers, "I know where she is, I know she's not coming back…and you will know how it feels now, to lose the one you love, to never be a parent, it all stops with us, and you know, that's for the best because you and me, we are damaged. Look at us…"

Dan pulled his face away from her hands and stood up, her words cut him, but she was right, they were both damaged.   "You drove her away. Did you pay her? Blackmail? She would never have left me."

"Darling, it really wasn't that difficult, it even surprised me…" She threw back her head and laughed. Dan shuddered. Laughs that don't come from happiness, are sinister and dangerous. This was that.   The laughter morphed into sobs.

"You're a piece of shit Colleen. We're done."

A naked Colleen grappled on the wet floor, sliding around as she tried to stand up. "Please don't leave. Not like this. I can't go on like it anymore."

Dan looked down at her, he wanted to call the doctor now, to get her sectioned. Show what a mess she was. But she had driven him to flip out and had the marks to prove it. She was close to breaking, and it would not be long before this could all be over. Her words were comforting, because she acknowledged her own desperation. But what did she know about Daisy? And if she knew anything, would she ever tell him anyway?

Dan turned away from his heap of a wife, grabbed his keys and slammed the front door against her wailing. "Dan! Come back! Please don't go!"

SHERRY

Sherry locked the garden gate behind her, dropped to the grass and tried to catch her breath. The sprint back through the woods, didn't seem to get any easier, and she flapped her hand in front of her face to try and cool her scarlet cheeks. Once her breath slowed, she headed across her garden into the house, for a shower.

The steaming water cleansed her aching body, and she relished the soft soapy wash against her skin. She felt devoid of human contact for so long, and it was as though something inside her awoke and craved touch. Wasn't she as deserving as everyone else? She was far from perfect, but believed deep down she was a decent person, with good intent. Not like Colleen, she was a depraved attention seeking bitch. She switched off the shower, thinking she could hear her doorbell ring. Who would be ringing her doorbell at this time of the evening? She blinked away flashbacks of past ominous knocks on the door.

She passed her discarded clothes on the floor and kicked them into a heap in the corner of the bedroom. They would need to be disposed of later. She would add them to her garden incinerator with some sage and dried lavender later and watch them burn.

The doorbell rang again, and then repeatedly. Her body stiffened, she was not used to visitors and suspicion led her to the bedroom window. Her shoulders tensed as she saw it was Dan. "I'm coming! I'm coming!" She wrapped her dressing gown around her body. Why was he here?

"It's me, Dan."

"Hey, sorry was in the shower."

"Can I come in? Sorry are you busy? I didn't think."

"Come on in, here sit down while I throw on some clothes." His breath smelt of alcohol. "Did you drive here?"

"Don't lecture me. Not tonight."

"Let me throw on some clothes, I'll be right back."

Dan nodded and gulped on the half empty whiskey bottle.

Sherry's heart pounded, what did that mean? Upstairs, she picked the discarded clothing off the floor, and put them into a black bag which she stuffed into her wardrobe. "Won't be a mo!" She pulled on some leggings, an oversized sweatshirt and scraped back her wet hair into a high ponytail.

"You look rough. And reek of alcohol."

"Thanks, brutally honest – exactly what you need from an employee."

Sherry smiled. "I didn't mean it like that." Her smile hid her fear.

"Been driving around for hours, and well, want some of this?" Dan thrust the bottle towards her. She pushed it away and shook her head. He hadn't been home yet, and she relaxed a little.

"You shouldn't be here really. Not like this. Go home Dan."

"I thought you would listen." He cradled the bottle for a moment before drinking from it again.

"I'm not sure what's going on, but I don't see how I can help?" She really wanted him to leave but equally didn't want to upset him. She felt conflicted.

"It's Daisy..."

"She's back?"

"If Daisy were back, would I look like this? Would I be here in this state?" he stood and pointed to his unshaven face and messed up hair. It was the first time she saw him riled. He became more attractive the more messed up he looked, and Sherry's stomach tumbled. She fought the overwhelming urge to pull him in close to her. He looked so vulnerable and yet so strong and unpredictable. He was all over the place.

"I think something has happened to her, maybe something bad."

Sherry took his hand and as she pulled them both onto the sofa, their knees knocked together. Her lounge was as snug as her kitchen, the furniture suddenly felt oversized and cramped. "What do you mean? Have you heard something?"

"Me and Colleen had the worst fight, and she told me that Daisy would never be coming back to me…. that she knows where she is but will never tell me."

Sherry kept her mouth firmly shut, terrified that she would say too much.

"She said that I would never know what it felt like to be a parent. It was weird, throwing that into conversation, felt odd. She told me that now, I knew how it felt, to lose the ones I love."

"Do you think Daisy could be pregnant? That she left you, and was pregnant when she left?"

Dan nodded; his raw eyes stared blankly. "Maybe? But Colleen knows something, I'm telling you. She knows what happened to Daisy." He drained the remaining whiskey and burped, "Scuse me." His words were becoming more slurry by the moment.

"Perhaps she paid her off?"

Dan shook his head. "Never, Daisy wasn't into that material shit, that was what finished us off, she wanted me for me, not all the strings, business and money that came with it."

"Okay, you are going to have to help me here, I am not sure what you are actually saying?"

"You've seen me with bruises, cuts?"

Sherry nodded.

"Well, what if she did something to Daisy? Something violent or threatened it at least? If she thought, if she knew Daisy was... I know what she is capable of, she loses her shit and it's like nothing you could imagine. She was desperate to be a mother, for years. And, well, if Daisy was pregnant, she could never have allowed that to happen...But why the fuck would Daisy not have told me? Why would she have left knowing she was having our child? It's all so fucked up, and the more I think about this, the darker my brain goes."

Sherry's focus wavered, and her heart fluttered. He chose to seek refuge with her. She could help him, look after him. She shifted forwards to hold him, and then pulled away. No, he needed to go home, him rocking up at her house, was only going to entangle her. "Dan, go home, ask Colleen. See if you can get it out of her, promise anything she wants for fucks sake."

Dan momentarily sobered up. "I've never heard you swear before. It sounds wrong. Shall I leave the car here, you don't mind, do you? Can't drive home in the state."

"Well, you arrived in this state." She wanted to tell him to drive it away, she didn't want his car parked outside her house. But figured that he would have been seen by someone. So, it really didn't make much difference. "Leave it here, you shouldn't drive."

He swayed in the doorway. "I'll promise her whatever I need to, to get the truth, right." He opened the door and staggered into a sloppy run, swaying on and off the pavement.

Sherry's brain swirled with possible paths, but her quick thinking untangled them enough to clear the way. The clothes. She sprinted upstairs, grabbed the bin bag and emptied it into the incinerator, a relic left over from her uncle's day. On top she emptied the brown paper bag full of dried lavender and sage. Sage was apparently cleansing, and lavender she hoped might be pungent to hide the smell of the clothing.

She grappled in the kitchen drawer for a box of matches and after lighting the first one, set fire to the whole box which she threw on top of the clothing and herbs. She watched the flames dance, confident that it was nothing unusual to burn garden stuff later in the evening, less disturbance to neighbours. This was the end of it. She was burning away the past.

Once the flames had done their work and nothing else was left except a few embers, distant sirens could be heard over the back of the woods. She cleared out the fire remnants, raking them into the soil of a flower bed and after watering the garden and moving the incinerator back to its original location, she locked up and crawled into bed. Suddenly, everything that unfolded that evening caught up with her, and she sank into a deep restorative sleep.

DAN

"I didn't kill her, when I left, she was screaming for God's sake. Why would I call the police on myself? I called you when I found her!"

"But you admit, you physically injured her?"

Dan nodded. "Yes! We've established that we fought, that's how I got my injuries, but I didn't kill her. Why are you only looking at me? No one in the village likes her!"

The larger of the two Police officers, Burton, turned over a series of photographs. "Let's see if we can identify anything you admit to inflicting, shall we? How about this one?" He pointed to bruising around the neck.

Dan glared at the gruesome image. He nodded. "Maybe, I don't know, I mean, whoever killed her could have done that."

"But you did, as you rightly pointed out earlier, squeeze her neck with your hands?"

Dan bowed his head. This was bad. They were never going to believe him, that he stopped the fight, and left. "CCTV? Did that show me leaving? Someone else arriving? Have you checked that?"

The officers exchanged exasperated glances. "Funnily enough, the CCTV wasn't working, hadn't been for a while by the looks of it. Coincidence?"

Dan was puzzled, why would it not be working? When did he last bother to check it? He couldn't remember looking at it for months. "I don't understand this."

"Come on Dan, this is stupid, why not admit it?"

"Because I didn't do it."

Burton lifted a box onto the table. "Okay, let's see what we have in here. One burner phone, recognise this?" He carefully placed a mobile phone encased in a plastic evidence bag, onto the table.

Dan swallowed, he knew they would turn the house upside down and if they did, this would be found. Another nail in his coffin. He nodded.

"And you used this for..."

"No comment."

"Dan, you used this for blackmailing your wife. Funny because the number you have dialled on this phone, no longer exists, must have got wind of you being in here…"

Dan chewed his fingernail.

"What about the large sums of money, your wife has been withdrawing from the bank account?"

He studied the bleeding skin around his cuticle, and then moved on to the next finger.

"What was the point? Trying to push her over the edge? Wouldn't divorce have been the easier option for all parties?"

Daisy. If only he had listened to her and got out all those months ago. Greed now shackled him to his ever-worsening fate. Nothing he could say could make this any better.

"What happened then, blackmail not working quick enough for you? Or did Colleen get out of hand, and it went too far this time, I mean, anger, seeing red, takes our control sometimes doesn't it. Is that what happened Dan?"

"I didn't kill her." Dan played over in his mind, the same question. Who killed Colleen? It had to be *them*? He couldn't mention names, not yet, not until he was desperate. Because if he grassed and got out, he would soon be joining Colleen on the other side. They wouldn't stand for that. Besides, no one really liked her, she pissed most of the village off at some point, it could be anyone? But he knew that was stupid, of course it couldn't be anyone – this wasn't a film and usually people don't just go around killing other people because they have an axe to grind.

"She isn't liked, have you asked around? Maybe she pissed someone off, shagged their husband or wife? Have you thought about that?"

"Okay, let's talk about your relationship. So did you and your wife engage in a full marriage?"

"No. Not for years."

"And that was by mutual agreement?"

Dan shook his head, "She still tried, I refused. Then we would fight. So, it was easier to avoid those situations."

"You had separate bedrooms?"

"Yes."

"And you never shared?"

"Not recently no, we did in the beginning when we were young."

"And you never engaged in a sexual way with her?"

"No."

"Because you had a mistress?"

"No, not because of that. Daisy isn't a mistress, I love her."

"I understand Colleen was a jealous person, so I imagine that was a hard pill for her to swallow, if you'll excuse the pun." Burtons mouth curled into a smile, self-satisfied with his joke. "We know about Colleen's habit."

"Obviously." Dan shifted in his chair. "We didn't have sex because she repulsed me."

"Right. So, can you explain why we found your semen in her stomach?"

Dan sighed, shut his eyes tight and wished it would all end. She had royally fucked him over. And what could he say? That he didn't have a choice. Because he could have pushed her off him, and he didn't. "No comment."

"So, on the night your wife is drowned, in *your* hot tub, full of your own fresh little swimmers, her body covered with injuries sustained by you, and by your own admission. And you, with a set of your own injuries too, expect us to believe that you had nothing to do with her murder?" The officer shook his head in despair. "Why don't you do us all a favour and admit it."

Dan remained silent.

"So, I ask you again, wouldn't divorce be an easier option? Is any amount of money worth all this misery?"

"I know that now, and if I could go back and change things..."

"You wouldn't murder your wife?"

"Stop putting words in my mouth. I didn't kill her." Dan licked his dry lips. "Please can I have more water?"

"One more thing before we break, the blackmail scheme you had going, what were they blackmailing her about? And who were they?"

"No comment. But I really need that water now."

Trent, the slender officer, switched off the tape. "Five minutes, then we are back on it."

SHERRY

Her mind was focussed. She had to support Dan, he had lost everything, and would need her now. The villagers were avoiding the shop. They all believed he murdered Colleen, and although she wasn't exactly everyone's favourite person, murder was murder. She even heard whisperings, that they were pinning Daisy's disappearance on him too. Poor guy.

Despite the increasing amount of stock she was binning each day, and the footfall at zero or thereabouts, Sherry dutifully and singlehandedly flew the flag of solidarity and opened the shop. The only person still frequenting was Joan.

"Dan wouldn't do something like that, he just wouldn't. They be mad to think he was capable of something like that. Colleen, she is another kettle of fish, loose cannon that en… and you say he was cut and bruised? Well, that proves how vicious she was, not that he finished her off…" Joan was off on one.

Sherry listened as she packed the groceries into Joan's tatty shopping bag. Grateful that her mind was on Dan, and not her. Now confident that had Joan known anything from her past, it would have come up by now. She wasn't one to sit on information like that.

"Oh, cuts and bruises, it was dreadful to see. Must have been a bad fight."

"Well, they haven't called me in. I should tell em what for, mind, if they do. And you, you told them the state he was in?"

Sherry nodded. "Yep, told them all about his stressed mood and how it was unusual for him to turn up at my door, that he had been drinking too."

"You mind you don't feed their silly ideas with your words - I know Dan and I bloody well know he wouldn't do something like this."

"I did say that too."

"Well, you keep on saying it. Because it's the truth girl. Folk round here have a short memory. He has done a lot for them over the years."

"I am not sure I can keep the shop open much longer, there is talk that it will need to be closed, pending investigations, they must be looking into his finances too."

Joan paled. "Close the shop! I've heard it all now! Well, that's it for me, I'm calling them when I get home. And what will I do about my shopping?"

"I can always help. You can write me lists and I can bring it round."

Joan slapped a ten-pound note on the counter, her rage prevented her from speaking further, and waved her stick in the air in goodbye, as she hobbled out of the shop.

Sherry sighed. She knew the shop was on borrowed time, because in the phone call from Dan, he advised her to keep trading until told otherwise. His solicitor had her number and would update her. He was so appreciative of her support and unwavering belief in him, he said he would be forever in her debt. Remembering the conversation made her stomach leap.

Devoid of customers, she wandered to the window, and took apart the display, which Colleen had once commanded her to create, and began to clean. It was time to put up the FINAL CLEARANCE sign in the window, so she filled the space with as much stock as she could, to entice the bargain hunters in. With every item she stacked, she knew how much Colleen would hate the look of it, but carried on safe in the knowledge that she wouldn't be swanning in through the door at any point, flicking her ponytail and throwing her weight about. That bitch was gone.

Clearing the shop, watching it shrink daily pecked at her inner peace. Perhaps she was the poisoned fish, polluting every pond in which she swam. Her brother was right, and she did stir trouble wherever she landed. This was supposed to be a fresh start, her new beginning, if only life was that simple. No, Colleen was the poisoned fish, and now she had drowned in her own poison, the waters could clear. Dan could serve his time, and when released could start a fresh too.

She worked hard to focus her mind, as taught in her months of therapy. To focus on what she wanted to achieve, and not let racing thoughts gallop away. But the pull of Colleen, was becoming stronger as the shop emptied, and there was less to keep her hands busy. What would happen once the shop closed, and she was left jobless. She squeezed her eyes shut and rubbed her hands slowly together. One day at a time, she repeated over and over, until the image of Colleen's red hair splayed in the bubbles of the jacuzzi, disappeared.

Sherry flicked the messages on her answerphone to play, and amongst the cold callers, was a message from the solicitors, asking her to call them. Her stomach lurched, the shop was going to close, and she was no longer allowed to enter the building. She needed to drop off the keys as soon as possible. Her hands shook and her face flushed, so she implemented her breathing and brought herself back down to a mild irritation. She would need to let Joan know and would visit her tomorrow.

She unlocked the small linen cupboard off the landing and lifted Dan's mug off the shelf. She smiled, that she thought to take it at the time, because now she would have no access to the shop. She hadn't washed it since he last used it and felt his energy bubble up, whenever she lifted it up to her mouth. Her fingers trailed along the soft, stained fabric of the white t-shirt, folded neatly on the shelf. She smiled and pulled out a photograph of Colleen, it was one from Wiki. She carried it into her bedroom, and placed it in an emptied brassy bowl, which usually held her makeup. She lit the photograph, and dropped it into the bowl, watching her face and hair burn away. "You cannot hurt him anymore."

DAN

Dan was sick of playing over the events in his mind, exhausted of the relentless questioning. He was going to be charged with murder for Christ's sake. He freely admitted to wanting to kill Colleen at times, daily sometimes. But he didn't kill her and the question he asked himself over and over was – who did? He was working on keeping away the increasing level of claustrophobia which seemed to intensify the more his dark thoughts circled. In a comedy or kids film he once saw, he couldn't remember the name, but a prisoner was rescued by blowing a hole in the cell wall, and then he simply hopped out the gap into the fresh air. He felt as though he couldn't breathe properly these days. He longed for a deep lung-full of country air.

His cell door swung open, and once again he was led to the interview room by a burly officer whose keys jangled as he walked. He was tired of the pretence and 'no comments', which seemed to prolong the whole process. This time, he would give the whole truth, lay all his cards out on the table. He was going down for her murder, so now, was the time to be honest and maybe there was hope that they may believe he was at least innocent of this, if willing to be honest about the blackmail.

The familiar flow of tape on and introduction complete, he shifted in his chair. His solicitor, Miles, beside him, would not be happy with the amount he was about to reveal, but he was paying him good money, and would have to swallow it.

"Dan, having gone through your official phone, we have found a file containing images of you with various injuries. Would you like to tell us about these?"

Miles had curly black hair and ruddy cheeks, which Dan suspected, evolved from one too many glasses of wine. But he was a good guy, and Dan trusted him. He tipped his head towards Dan and whispered, "You don't have to answer."

Dan waved him away. "Yes, actually, I would like to elaborate. I already told you Colleen was abusive. It was a toxic relationship, and I began to keep a record of my injuries, which I always excused in public as minor mishaps."

"You were blackmailing her. Weren't you?"

Miles leaned in, but before he could speak, Dan interjected, "Yes. I was blackmailing her. Well not directly. And not with these pictures."

Trent and Burton sat back and gently nudged each other, they were getting somewhere. Dan watched a smug smile creep onto Trent's face. His mop of brown hair needed a good cut, and he appeared as though he had got up out of bed in a hurry. "Go on."

Dan wanted to chuckle, they really thought they were calling the shots, in reality he was only telling them what he had already decided to do so. He stared at a sprawling circle of what appeared to be splashed coffee, faded into the tired walls. The harsh strip lights illuminated every scuff and stain, as if reminding whoever was in the 'hot seat' answering the questions, that they were scum.

"Dan, I really would like a quick word, before you say anything further." Mile's flushed face, implored Dan to shut his mouth.

But he touched his arm and shook his head. "No need Miles. I got this now. Please let me speak."

Miles gesticulated with his hands but said nothing more.

"Colleen's money began our business. I had nothing, and in the beginning, we were good, me and her. So, we set it up as a joint venture, she kept control with me, she as the funder, and I was going to run it. Her drugs started early in her modelling days, but she was clean initially when we first got married, I wasn't into that shit." He clicked the joints in his fingers one at a time and swallowed.

"And?"

"To cut a long story short, life with her is intolerable. She is... was... selfish and volatile and oh, let's not forget the violence."

"Let's not forget that you are also capable of violence Dan." Burton, the older, balding officer pointed accusingly at Dan, and wagged his finger like a headmaster scolding a pupil. He made Dan want to shut down and say nothing more. Patronising fuckwit.

"Anyway, I decided enough was enough," Dan continued, determined to keep this on track and as close to in control as anyone can manage in police custody. "After Daisy left, she was the only thing that kept me sane, I decided there were only two ways out, kill Col, or send her to the brink of sanity, or at least make it look that way."

Miles squirmed in his seat; Dan flicked him a wry smile. The officers watched him intently, wide eyed.

"I never could have killed her, despite her making my life a living hell. So instead, I followed her to one of her meetings with her dodgy acquaintances, and then approached them. Offered them money, if they blackmailed her."

"Blackmailed her about what?"

"Well, that was the thing, she was back using again, but that wouldn't be enough to extort much from her, not for long. But that was the beginning. The test. Started off with small amounts. Then they ramped it up. Caught her on one of her overtly sexual days, took some questionable photos after sampling a little too much of the white stuff. That was when it shifted gear. Threatened to leak the photos online. Send them to me. You know, that kind of thing."

"You pimped your wife out? That's basically what you are saying."

"My wife did not need persuading, and from the looks of the photographs was having a very enjoyable time." Dan sighed and leant back into the chair. "She had no idea I already knew. Was desperate for us to try for a baby. Lunacy. Try for a baby, I would never have trusted her as a mother, she was a fucking monster!"

"So, it was this need for a baby, which fuelled the payments, the need to hide the truth? How?"

"Because, I had told her, co-incidentally, that one more infidelity and it was over and there would never be any hope for a baby. Let me be clear, there was never any hope for a baby, because we never had sex, not for a long time. But in her deluded mind, she tried often, thought I would cave eventually. So, to her this threat was real. A showstopper. But as our relationship deteriorated, I think her hopes faded, and so did her willingness to pay their demands. They told me that they had something else big to lay at her door. But I never found out what it was."

"We have witnesses to say that you were aggressive towards Colleen, only weeks before her death. That you were throwing your weight about regarding money which was missing from an account?"

He smiled. "Aha, you must mean the hot tub incident. The gaggle of women drinking my champagne, using my house as though it was a hotel? Yes, I did. All part of my plan you see. Needed her to believe I wasn't in on it, to add more stress. Now I could pressure her about the missing money, and *they* would be squeezing more out of her too. Few people would not crack under that pressure, and that was all I needed – her to crack, so that I could get all the papers in order, control of everything I had worked so fucking hard to build despite her, and...well find Daisy. I admit that I wanted her to crack, lose her mind, but I DID NOT kill her."

SHERRY

Sherry awoke in a pool of sweat. Her dreams were filled with *that* night, it was as though her brain was checking for DNA residue, or evidence she had been there. She knew there would be none, and if anyone had seen her leaving, she would know about it by now. In her interview with the police, she opted for the honesty method, and immediately told them about her fresh start, and previous 'issues', which they were appreciative of. She seemed to satisfy their questions with her carefully constructed answers, which seemed to innocently implicate Dan in Colleen's demise.

She was his one connection outside of custody now, and they were imminently awaiting his charge of murder, which may be dropped to manslaughter, because of his evidence of previous harm by Colleen and the injuries which he also sustained on the night. They were not looking elsewhere. They had everything they needed.

Her powerful mind often recalled the expertly executed blow job, which Colleen forced on Dan, and the fight which ensued. Her blood would boil at the recollection, and the anger. She hadn't planned to kill her, but watching Colleen's drug-induced sleepiness take hold, and the fact that she was in the water, meant it was easy to push her head under, and except for a few splashes, it was quiet and uneventful beneath the jets of the tub. Medusa flame hair on the surface of the water; an image burned into her memory. But once her body stilled, Sherry crept away, having touched nothing but the chlorinated water and Colleen's head beneath it.

Sherry heard afterwards that the cameras on the property were not working at the time, but she had skilfully avoided being seen by them anyway. It was easy to do if you knew how.

She showered and then headed over to see Joan. She would need to get her shopping sorted, and support Joan through everything that was going on with Dan. Poor Joan, she really thought the world of Dan. This would be destroying her.

Sherry pushed through the rickety gate and wandered up the gravel path to the front door. The garden was immaculate, and not a blade of grass appeared out of place. Varying rose bushes and large purple hydrangeas lined the pathway. Even her windows gleamed as if they were washed daily. The knocker was loud and purposeful, useful for an old person with hearing issues, although she was unaware Joan suffered in this way. A face peered through the net curtain, before the door opened. "The shops not open, that's why you're here."

"Can I come in Joan?"

Joan stood holding the door open only slightly, as though debating whether to allow Sherry passage into her home. Sherry smiled; her face puzzled by Joans reluctance.

"Spose." Joan swung open the door. "Don't get many in here these days."

"Its very tidy, and your garden, that must be a labour of love."

"Hmm."

They lingered in the hallway, Joan stood firm at the entrance to the lounge. "I was thinking that I could get my own shopping, will go to the other shop. They've been talking about expanding their stock, since this business began with Dan. So already have the basics, and that's all I need, nothing much. So, I thank you for your offer of help, which is why, I assume you are here, but I don't need it."

Sherry opened her mouth and then closed it again. She wasn't sure why this conversation shocked her, because Joan didn't mince her words- ever. And yet she felt hurt and misunderstood.

"I didn't want Dan to worry about you, that's all."

"Don't you think he has more to worry about than me? He won't be thinking about me. I have managed ok all my life, and I still will. I don't need you meddling."

"Joan, you must be upset by everything that's going on..."

"Don't presume to know what does or doesn't upset me. You don't know me, and just because you have served me in a shop doesn't make us friends. I should be glad if you were to remember that."

Sherry was lost for words, but only for a moment. "It's okay, I understand – it's so hard right now, but know, when you need me, I will be here. This is my number and all you need to do is call me." Sherry held out a piece of paper, but Joan stared at it, refusing to take it.

Sherry placed it next to the telephone on the stand, by the little window. "It's there anyway. I will leave you in peace now."

"Bit late for that isn't it? Peace? Things seem all topsy-turvy since you moved into that house. I see more than you think missy, not as naïve as Dan nor blinkered by flattery. You don't get to my age without learning a thing or two."

Sherry's eyes narrowed. "I am not sure what you are implying, but I think you have got me wrong. I only came over to see if I could help you. That's all."

Joan opened the door. "Goodbye Sherry."

The door closed before she could clear the frame, it caught her foot. "Ouch! Fuck that hurt!" She limped up the path and closed the gate. "What a stupid old bitch."

DAN

For fucks sake, can't a man sleep? Haven't you asked me enough questions today? He was back in the same interview room, no doubt to be asked the same questions. "You want to get a better cleaner in here, that smear across the glass has been on there since I arrived."

With the tape and usual introductions over, they wasted no time to begin.

"Dan Sullivan, we have some final questions to ask you, before we are to formally charge you with the murder of your wife, Colleen Sullivan."

Dan gasped, "but I told you everything. I was completely honest!"

"On searching your premises, it appears a second body has been found. Do you have anything to say about that?"

Dan reeled. What the fuck? A second body? It was bad enough there was a first. "Look, this is some sick fucking game you are playing."

"It would appear to be the body of a pregnant female, and she is yet to be formally identified. Do you have anything to say about this?"

Dan said nothing, but his stomach lurched. Daisy? His face paled, and the room spun. He felt sick.

"We also found a phone, in your wife's bedroom, registered to Daisy Grey. And at present we are accessing the phone records of the account, to see if we can shed some light."

"You think the body is Daisy?" Tears blurred his vision, and he suddenly felt penned in, the need to escape. His breathing sped up, his nostrils flared, and blood surged through his veins.

"We have officers working on this as we speak. For the tape, please can you confirm if you have any knowledge of this body in your garden prior to this conversation."

"Dan?" Miles tapped his arm to break the trance he appeared to be locked into.

"No. No fucking idea. If that's Daisy...why would she have come to the house?" Dan was rambling, and Miles was conscious the tape was still rolling.

"Dan…"

"Colleen, it had to be her. She must have lured her there…"

Dan jumped to his feet and shoved the table with such force, that the officers sat across from him yelped. "That fucking bitch! She got what she deserved, karma! She's taken everything from me!"

He punched the table until his knuckles bled. Miles attempted to calm him down but stood away, whilst two back-up officers fought to cuff him. The knee in his back pinned him to the floor, as he screamed, "You fucking bitch Colleen!" He writhed and jerked. "Get the fuck off me!"

"Dan, you're making it worse. You must stop this." Mile's words were futile, and Dan continued to struggle, lashing out with his legs. His mind spun and his brain refused to accept that he would never see Daisy again. Consumed with hate and anger, the only person he could think about was Colleen, and how he wished he had been the one to have finished her off. She deserved it all.

When he woke up, his whole body ached. He creaked his neck and stretched his arms straight, groaning. His intense pain afforded him a moment of ignorance. It was as though his memory was rebooting- catching up, because his first thought was acknowledging the various places he hurt and gingerly trying to move. It was only after a few seconds that he remembered. Daisy was dead. Colleen killed her. What the fuck was going on? He launched himself off the hard bed, towards the door and pounded it. "I want to speak to my brief! Get my fucking brief NOW!"

SHERRY

Sherry stared into the empty shop window and slowly turned her head from side to side. The reflection surpassed expectation: she licked her lips and smiled, confident that she had never looked so good. The crisp white shirt and navy wide-legged trousers were a change to her normal style but fitted perfectly with her shorter blonde bob.

Now Dan had been charged and was awaiting trial, she needed to give him something to think about inside. She wanted him to see her differently, to feel grateful for her loyalty, but to be attracted to her, so that maybe they could one day be together. Of course, it would be a long way off, his court case wasn't until later in the year, and who knows what sentence they would give him. She could only hope that they would not go along with the latest theory, that he planned to kill Colleen, because he found out about Daisy. She hoped it would have been seen as a crime of passion. She brushed his letter over her lips, and pushed it into the post box, and headed home, past the pub.

"Sherry!" A voice called from the upstairs of the pub. "Hold on, I'm coming down."

Sherry waited in the car park for Jackie to reach her. She was out of breath and signalled with her finger for Sherry to give her a moment to recover.

"Do you know how Dan is?" Her face was red from exertion. "Smokey and I wanted to visit or write to him? Do you think he would like that? We don't believe he could have killed anyone; I know they had a turbulent relationship, and she was a piece of work, but murder, Dan? No."

"Well, you know he really was in love with Daisy, and Colleen was jealous of anyone who went near him."

Jackie's eyes narrowed. "So, you believe he may have done it?"

"I'm not saying that. It's..."

"You have known Dan a couple of months; we have known them both for years. And I do not believe he would kill anyone." Jackie's words cut Sherry off, and her stern face stared at her.

Sherry switched her tone to soft, and touched her arm. "Oh, you have misread what I am saying, I totally agree. Dan is kind and gentle."

Jackie's face relaxed a little. "So, what about visitors?"

"He doesn't want visitors, too ashamed. And he also told me that he doesn't want anyone writing to him either, he doesn't want pity." She shrugged her shoulders, almost believing her own lie.

"Oh." Jackie's eyes teared with her deflated answer. "That's sad, I thought he may want some supporters."

Sherry squeezed Jackie's hand, and she scrunched up her face in sympathy. "It's tough isn't it, I mean, it's like living in a nightmare really. I loved that job too."

"Of course, you have lost your job- I didn't even think. Well, if you would ever like some shifts behind the bar, I am sure we could use some help."

Sherry beamed. "That's so kind. Thank you. I will bear that in mind. Now I must head off as I have something on, but lovely to speak to you. Thanks again."

Sherry turned away and headed down the country lane towards home. She hoped her performance had been enough to prevent Jackie from contacting Dan, she needed to be his world now. And that could only happen the more isolated he felt.

As she bustled about the cottage, plumping cushions and dusting the windowsill, her mind crept to Colleen. She still couldn't believe what lows she would stoop to. What a bitch, how could anyone kill a pregnant woman? And then to bury her in the copse at the

121

bottom of their own garden. To think that for all those months Dan had been wondering where Daisy was, and trying to contact her, and she was only a short walk away the whole time! Crazy.

She checked her watch as her doorbell rang. They were on time. She paused a moment to breathe, rubbing her hands together and pulling her shoulders back. This was her moment.

"Hi, I'm Sherry, please come in." Her face displayed a smile but her eyes remained narrowed.

The reporter was alone, which was a surprise. "Hi Sherry, David, Evening Post. Thanks for agreeing to meet with me."

"No worries, David, would you like a hot drink?"

"Coffee would be amazing. White, with two please."

"Sure, take a seat in the sitting room, unless you would like to sit outside? I only have a rickety bench though."

"In here is fine, I'll get sorted, thanks."

Sherry mindlessly put their coffees together, suppressing the smile which repeatedly crept to her lips. She didn't want to appear jovial, considering the situation, and furrowed her brow, reminding herself to think before she answered. She had toyed with declining the interview, wondering if it would draw too much attention to her. But once the charge was made on Dan, she knew no one was looking her way, and it was only for the local paper. It might be fun.

She placed both cups onto a tray and chewed her lip as she walked the tiny distance into the lounge. "Here, hope it's not too strong."

"Cheers. So…" David took a sip but scowled and placed it on the coffee table, it was too hot.

Sherry perched on the edge of the armchair and flicked her new hair from her face.

"You worked for the Sullivans, for how long?"

"Four months, but I only met Colleen less than a handful of times. It was Dan I knew really."

"And Dan, did he ever lead you to believe he could be capable of murder?"

Sherry took a slow sip of coffee, and stalled, remembering her own advice, not to rush her answers. "No. I always felt comfortable with him.

He did seem, vulnerable I guess, like she made his life difficult."

"Can you elaborate?"

"Well, he often had cuts, bruises. He would always explain them away, but I began to think it was more than that. And of course, now we know it was her. He seemed exhausted, like he was carrying a huge burden."

"Do you think he could have planned this murder? That Colleen could have told him about Daisy, and he lost it. That's what everyone is saying."

Sherry hid her smile with her mug. She swallowed her initial words, before speaking. "No. I don't think Dan had any idea that she killed Daisy. No one did. I think that she probably went too far, that in self-defence he lost his rag. He wouldn't have intended to."

"And Daisy, what do you know about that?"

"Only that Dan thought she was in Portugal. He still wasn't over her. It seems to be the perfect crime of passion. Wife drives mistress away, husband loses his rag, wife... well you know how the story ends."

David nodded. He had opted to record their interview, but he had questions neatly typed out in a folder.

"There was something else, I mean I have told the police this information too. When I first moved here, I witnessed Colleen and a biker guy, leathers, all the gear, in the woods beside here. I didn't know who she was then, not until I met her again at the shop. They appeared to be having an altercation, and I guess now, it must have been the people who were blackmailing her."

"Could you identify this guy?"

"Already done so, with the police, like a photo-fit type thing. He also came into the shop too, so guessing he knew both Dan and Colleen but in what way I haven't figured it out yet."

DAN

Dan's brain was permanently reeling. He had given up closing his eyes and hoping it was all a nightmare, because this was his life now. He had not murdered anyone and couldn't work out where it had all gone wrong.   He would be waiting months for trial, and in the meantime was rotting away in a grotty prison, with itchy sheets and sloppy food. The occasional letter from either Joan or Sherry was his only interaction with the outside world, except for his visits from Miles. Sherry wanted to visit, but he had so far kept that at bay, he couldn't face her in person.

Everything always came back to the same fact, Daisy was dead. Colleen killed her and effectively that meant it was his fault. He failed to protect her and their unborn child. What a fuck up.

Nothing could make this ok. Even if they started looking in a different direction, and searching for an alternative narrative, Daisy would still be dead, and his business fucked. His reputation which he spent so long protecting and building was in tatters. There was nothing worth living for. Yet he was still alive. He wished he wasn't.

Sherry had filled him in about what the village were saying, and that even Jackie and Smokey from the pub had turned on him. Sherry wrote affectionate and encouraging letters, but they were empty words, and the idea of a world without Daisy was unthinkable.

Sherry had given the police a description of biker guy, and they had issued a photo fit. That was not good news, for either of them. His mind pulled a fact from the depths of his memory, a telephone conversation where they said that they had something 'bigger' on Colleen, to use as blackmail. It must have been Daisy. Fuck, unknowingly, he even had a hand in Daisy's murder, his heavies, using it against Colleen to extort money, to send her mad...

He could not get his head around the idea that Daisy, and their unborn child, had lay in the copse at the bottom of his garden...blood rushed to his head, and it felt as though it might explode. He had nowhere to direct the pent-up anger, Colleen was dead already. And he was alone in a concrete cage, with no way out. He threw himself to the floor and began a round of push-ups, harder and faster than he had ever managed before. And every time he got to 50, he started again. He spat out every number, forcing away dark thoughts and concentrating only on reaching 50, over and over.

Eventually, his arms refused to co-operate, and he spun onto his back, wiping his face with his sleeve. He was sweat-soaked and breathing heavily and fast.

Sherry had no clue what she had done by co-operating with the police about the biker. *They* would not take it well and she would be in danger once they found out, or worse, *he* would be if they suspected him of grassing. Fucking hell, it was all spiralling, and he was on the edge. He would be stupid to think they had no reach inside. If they wanted to get him, they would. His only hope was that they would know it wasn't him who spilled.

How had his world gone from successful businessman, albeit in a miserable marriage, but a good life, to this. Nothing. He had nothing. Why had he chosen the path he had? Greed. Why had he lost Daisy? Greed, because he was unable to let go of a business which was lost now anyway. Why was he in prison? The answer to that question went around his head and there was only one conclusion: someone had set him up. But who? This alone, was the only thing stopping him from ending it all.

He wanted to find out who killed Colleen. It puzzled him. He didn't even care anymore, what fate lay ahead for him, but the idea that someone finished her off, at his house, in his hot tub plagued him. Especially as he had become the fall guy.   Perhaps it was *them*? Maybe they no longer wanted to play nice, thought the money was drying up? But that didn't make any sense, she was a cash cow. And now there was no more money. So, no. Not them. But who? Suicide? Accidental? They ruled that out because of the injuries. But he caused them, and she was very much alive, when he left the house. So maybe they should re-look at suicide as a real possibility? There was no way they would listen to him, but she was on the edge, and her mind unstable, so to him it was possible, that she did it to herself.

He jumped to his feet, peeled off his soaked sweatshirt and paced the cell, muttering ideas, trying to untangle the jumbled thoughts and make sense of what was happening.

The envelope caught his eye on the small table, it was Joans writing, and he had not yet bothered to read it. He stopped pacing and took the letter to his bed. Leaning his back against the cold wall, he drew his legs into his chest and opened the letter, written in perfect cursive handwriting:

Dear Dan,

You are still so missed. I can't imagine how hard this is for you. When I heard about poor Daisy, I wept for all the cruel things I have said about her disappearing. She was a lovely young lady, and I can't imagine what her final moments must have been like.

So, with trepidation, because my previous assumptions about poor Daisy were unfounded and I feel I should have learnt a lesson about jumping to conclusions, I find my thoughts hard to write. So, I will not say much, but have enclosed an article which I recently found in the local newspaper. It feels odd. That's all I shall say, because you must read it and then make your own sense of it. I wonder if you should be careful in trusting a certain person.

Just know, I do not believe you killed Colleen.

With love and thanks for all you have ever done for me,

Joan xxx

Perplexed, Dan pulled the newspaper cutting from the envelope. A picture of Sherry, looking completely different, sat alongside an article headlined:

DIRTY DAN IN CRIME OF PASSION

SHERRY

Sherry examined the newspaper article again. She had cut it out of 3 separate copies, in case the original got damaged. It looked as bad as the first 20 times she read it. The article was full of mis-quotes and implication. She had not come off well. The only silver lining was her photograph, and for once she was pleased with how she looked; unrecognisable from before. Initially, when David suggested a photo, she fought off the panic, and possibly would have refused if it was going any further than the locality. But her vanity got the better of her, and she agreed. On seeing the result, she was glad she did, because she looked pretty good. Shame the words were not so kind. David had come across as professional and trustworthy, but she should have known he would twist it all and focus on the wrong stuff. She needed to be more savvy. What a nerdy little bastard.

Joan was bound to get on her case now, as the article implied that Sherry thought Dan was guilty. In some ways that was good, because no one was looking her way, all the time the narrative was: DIRTY DAN IN CRIME OF PASSION. People loved a good crime of passion. It would catch on and become truth in no time, like some kind of urban myth. That's how they begin, with stories being told. Say something enough times and it becomes truth. Anyway, she could deal with an annoying, little old lady like Joan. No one gave a shit about her, no one knew if she were alive or dead. That's what happens when you become a twisted old gossip.

Jackie's offer for some shifts at the pub, were appealing to her new confident self. Perhaps that was exactly what she needed, and it would at least bring a small amount of income in too. She decided to call in later, and have a drink, enquire whilst there. It was a bold move for the Sherry who first arrived in the village, but the new version was strutting forwards into her new persona.

It was seven when she arrived, and they were serving dinner to families, who were probably holidaying and staying at the campsite. A small terrier sat obediently next to his family, waiting for a scrap or two no doubt. As she walked towards the bar, he launched at her feet and his snarls erupted into incessant barking. "Stop it Roly, what is the matter?" The embarrassed owners swooped to put on his lead and pull him away. "So sorry, he's never like this usually."

"It's fine, I expect I startled him when I came in that's all, eh Roly?"

The dog replied with a tooth-baring snarl, as his owners led him around the far side of their table in the hope they could finish their dinner in peace, whispering embarrassed but inaudible dialog.

"Hey Jackie, vodka and coke please."

"Ice?"

Sherry nodded and tried to ignore the ongoing kerfuffle with Roly behind her, as he refused to settle back down.

"You okay?"

Jackie smiled, but it was the one she saved for the punters whom she disliked but must be professionally friendly with. Sherry had been on the receiving end of those, from many different people for years, and could tell them a mile away.

"£4.20 please?"

Sherry handed over a five-pound note. "Thanks. I will sit over in the corner if that's ok?"

"That's reserved from 8, but fine for now."

Sherry sat far away from the table with the annoying dog and sank into the comfy armchair. She questioned why she hadn't been there more often. It was a lovely country pub; tastefully kitted out too, with industrial fittings, mis-matching furniture and sanded floorboards. She could imagine bustling about behind the bar and chatting with people. She would need to practise her own professional smile too, for all the fuckwits who would inevitably frequent the pub.

She smiled, confident that she could now settle properly, that her past wasn't going to come looking for her in this tiny village, where nothing much ever happened. Except for a murder or two. She shouldn't joke about these things, not even to herself, because Daisy didn't deserve to die, that was tragic. But Colleen was a drain on everyone in her vicinity. She was sucking the life out of poor Dan. Fought and

134

killed a pregnant woman and an all-round bitch to anyone who crossed her path...she was a piece of work. If she hadn't helped her along, she would have probably drowned anyway, she was that half-cut.   If only she hadn't had the injuries from her fight with Dan, they would have seen it as an accident. That was what she thought would happen. She shivered.

"Smokey told me not to say anything, but there it is."

Sherry looked up at a red-faced Jackie, looming over the table. "What's up?"

Jackie let out an exacerbated laugh, but kept her voice low, to avoid disturbing the customers. "You really don't know?"

Sherry shook her head and took a sip of her drink which she then cradled in her hand.

"The article in the newspaper? "

"Oh, I see. Well to be honest they didn't print it quite how it was. I felt a bit surprised when I first read it too."

"You threw Dan under the bus!"

"I just told the truth."

"You implied he was capable of murdering Colleen. He wouldn't."

"She was injured, and so was he. They fought. There was no escaping the facts!"

"Do you know how many reporters have sat in my pub, and how many we've refused to talk to? Well, I can't count how many, but a lot, because friends don't do that. We thought you cared for Dan. That you were a friend of his. How do you think he would feel?"

Sherry felt her face flush, and anger rise but fought to keep it down, and swallowed hard. She needed to be clever, pretend she was sorry even though she felt only irritation. "Oh Jackie, I never thought of it like that, I feel terrible now." She dabbed at her dry eyes with a tissue from her handbag. "What must you both think of me?"

Jackie's stance softened a little, and sympathy pursed her lips. "Rookie error? Never talk to any journo's because they always twist what you say."

Sherry sniffed away imaginary tears and finished the remains of her drink. "I feel so stupid now."

136

Jackie squeezed her hand. "He's got such little support around here. That's all. He needs his friends. Well, the few he has left anyway."

Sherry nodded. "I know I haven't been here long, and that Dan and I don't have history, not like you and Smokey, but he has confided in me, because of that very reason. I think because I am unconnected to everyone here, that's why he could and still opens-up to me."

"Let me get you another drink, on the house." Jackie winked at her.

Sherry watched her check in on the feasting families en route to the bar, clearing plates and dirty napkins away. Jackie seemed to have bought her tears. She had underestimated the power of a little newspaper article and the bad feeling it could cause. And she needed to remember how protective of Dan they felt here in the pub. Other than that, her plan was working, and she hoped they would agree on when her first shift would be before she left.

DAN

Grey, monotonous and unbearable. His days bled into one long nightmare. His only highlight was his letters from Joan, which held some snippet of normality. He had paused answering Sherry's as he was trying to get his head around the newspaper article. It was strange and it felt wrong. But he couldn't work it out. She appeared to be metamorphosising into a new person, one he didn't recognise from the bland reliable shop assistant who first approached him for a job. He needed to think about it all.

His weekly letters arrived, and he left Sherry's on the table but opened Joans. A second also appeared to be in the same envelope but he didn't recognise the writing. He scanned the page and saw it was signed from Jackie. With a puzzled face, he turned the letter back over and begun reading:

Dear Dan

I hope you don't mind me writing to you, I have wanted to for a while, but Sherry advised me that was not your wish. So, I held off until it was no longer possible. I approached Joan and she agreed to

sending this with hers, as I really want to get in touch with you.

I have Sherry working a few shifts at the pub now. I can tell you that I am doing this out of my suspicions towards her. She seems to be acting in a strange way, and somewhat erratically. I have a bad feeling about her. I know Joan sent you a copy of the article she was involved with in the newspaper, and since then she seems to be in some weird transition into someone Smokey and I do not recognise.

I wondered if you have any background information about her? Did she give you any references or anything which we could look into? Where she came from, what her previous jobs were? Or family? Joan knew her uncle, but he was estranged from his family, and rarely talked about them, so that's no use. If you can write back with any information, please do, and we will try and gather what facts we can. I don't know what all of this means, but I am following my instincts.

I hope you are surviving in there. For the record, I believe you to be innocent. I know things were a mess between you and Colleen, that you both were at fault and guilty of questionable things within your marriage, but you are not a murderer. Not like Colleen, although I have to say that came as a shock.

We were so sorry to hear about poor Daisy. The village is organising a memorial service for her on Sunday, so I will light a candle for you.

One last thing, if you are still writing to Sherry, please don't let her know Joan and I are in touch, we are hoping to catch her off-guard, and I am not letting on to her that I have written to you either.

I look forward to hearing from you soon and stay strong.

With love

Jackie & Smokey

The letter dropped to his lap, and tears of relief sprung to his eyes, someone believed him and wanted to help. His thoughts began shooting off in new directions, that maybe there was a chance he could fight this, prove his innocence. Then he remembered the heavy circumstantial evidence which outweighed everything.

He gave up swallowing his tears, as they weren't for himself, but for Daisy and his unborn baby. A memorial service made it all seem real. She was gone and so was his future, he failed them both. "I'm sorry my love." He whispered into the air and repeatedly banged the back of his head against the wall, trying to feel pain from the numbness which prison induced.

The unexpected letter was full of information. And gave him so much to think about. He re-read the part about Sherry and her references and tried to remember the outcome. He knew that they had discussed it, because he was always hot on them from any new employees regardless of which part of the business they were involved in or level of their role. But he couldn't remember it going any further. It was back when things began to spiral. Daisy was missing, Colleen was playing up and he was run ragged, so maybe he let it slip. But that did mean he had nothing to go on. He had allowed a stranger, who blew in on the wind from God-knows-where, into his business. What the fuck was he thinking? She could have been bleeding him dry for months, and would he even have noticed? A sudden unease crept across him. He would ask Miles to dig around, see what he could find out.

He was glad that Joan and Jackie were in touch now. They made a good team and were his only shot of ever having the truth uncovered. He would write back to them, and to Sherry a benign thanks, just to keep her erratic thoughts in tow.

SHERRY

Sherry placed her sunglasses on her face, and satisfied that her look was complete, left the house on foot towards the church. Secretly she was representing Dan at the memorial service, she had told him this in her letter. And she carried with her a posy of white and gold gerberas, to leave by the bench in the cemetery, which would later be dedicated to Daisy in the ceremony.   She was delighted with the glamourous 'Jackie O' look she had pulled off and felt she had done Dan proud.

The mournful tone of the church bells reverberated through her core, and she felt absorbed in the moment, ignoring the whispering of the villagers, and backs being turned, due to her connection with the

142

accused. She maintained her composure and sat tall on an empty pew near to the front, staring at the large, framed photograph, of a smiling young woman. Daisy was pretty, in a freckly and had lovely white teeth. It was a good photo of her, better than the ones she had previously seen. But Sherry was surprised that she was Dan's type.

As the service began, she realised her pew remained empty except for herself. She turned around, and all eyes darted away, to look anywhere but at her, except for one pair. Joans. She stared directly at Sherry, as if in defiance to the others. Sherry narrowed her eyes, until she realised it was a futile gesture as her shades still sat on her face. She turned back towards the altar, and reminded herself that she was doing this for Dan, and she did not give a flying fuck, what any of these village misfits felt about her.

She sang and prayed the loudest, playing the part of professional mourner perfectly. What a shame Daisy's family did not attend the service, because she would have loved to offer them her sincerest condolences.

Sherry arrived at work as Jackie was making coffee. "Want one?"

Sherry shook her head; Jackie's coffee was vile and not a patch on what she was used to drinking. "Is it the same one you normally use? Because if so, no thanks."

Jackie smiled, "You don't like my coffee then?"

"So, what do you have planned for me today?"

"Well, the tables need a wipe from lunch, it was a busy one. And a general tidy up, then you can serve if that's ok?"

Sherry nodded. "And this is all under your watchful eye I am guessing?"

"Of course! You are technically still a trainee after all."

She winced, a trainee? Her anger threatened to choke her. She coughed and then used her professional smile. "Oh yes, I feel much more comfortable when you're on hand anyway. It's all new to me still."

Sherry sauntered over to the tables and began wiping, aware of Smokey and Jackie's low mutterings. Who did they think they were? She practically ran the shop for Dan. Serving a few drinks behind a bar was not exactly taxing on her brain, but then again, she was lucky to have been offered the hours, they didn't have to do that. She smiled, a proper smile of gratitude and knuckled down.

It was a slow evening, having had a busy lunch service before she arrived. Smokey was his usual quiet self towards her, but Jackie was particularly engaging.

"So, you heard much from Dan? How he's doing? Did you tell him about the memorial service?"

Sherry leant against the bar. "He's not so good to be honest. His letters are regular but sparse. Although I guess there isn't much goes on in prison, so not much to report. I expect he was pretty cut up to miss the memorial service for Daisy."

Jackie nodded. "Do send him our love, when you next write to him."

"Of course, I always do." Sherry lied.

"So, where did you say you lived before here? I'm sure you told me, but my menopausal brain fog is always losing me information!" Jackie pulled a silly face.

Sherry paused, she didn't want it to feel as though she was hiding her past, but equally did not want to give anything away. "A long way from here, a place where no one matters to anyone."

Jackie frowned, and Sherry berated herself for the weird answer. "Not far from Dartmoor." It was the correct region, without being precise and she hoped this was enough to satisfy Jackie.

"Ooh lovely, although I'm surprised about your theory, about people not caring. Perhaps that was only your perception. Perhaps they cared but you didn't see it."

So, now she's a therapist too, not a very good one either. Sherry's professional smile was back, but she was aware that she was working a little too hard at it, and it felt more like a sneer. "Possibly."

A group of young farmers arrived, and Jackie slipped out the back to fire up the ovens for their chips, leaving her to serve, and dodge their conversation about her past, which felt more like a probe.

DAN

Ever since the memorial service, 4pm was a moment he honoured Daisy daily. It was stupid. Pointless. But it was all he could think of to offer, as he was unable to attend her funeral or any of her memorials. He would stop whatever futile activity to pass the time he was doing, and spend time thinking about her, apologising. It was a habit that he would find hard to break, as it became like a disrespect if he failed to observe it.

Joan had kindly sent him a picture of the bench which was dedicated to her memory, and he vowed one day to take flowers to her grave and her bench and honour her properly.

Sherry had been writing more frequently and sometimes her letters said little, and other times incessant ramblings about the pub, and how insulting Jackie and Smokey were about him, how hard it was to work there, but that she had no choice. Of course, he knew the truth, because Jackie fed him every detail back. Jackie felt as though Sherry was a pressure cooker that was building, and eventually she would explode.

147

Miles was on the case looking for information, and Dan had put him in touch with Smokey too, who he trusted implicitly. What would be unearthed was a mystery, but something about Sherry was off and somehow, he felt like time was running out. He couldn't explain this hunch. He wondered if it was because he had so much time to think. Thoughts were so powerful, you had to be aware of which ones to run with, and which to ditch. You could lose your shit easily and many did.

He decided to block the thought of his unborn child, it was too painful. Losing Daisy was devastating, but to know that his greed also ended his child's life? No, he couldn't allow himself to think any longer about that. His sole focus would be Daisy. That was too much to bear and enough anguish for two lifetimes anyway.

He still dreamed of her, as though she were still alive and calling him, but a dark shadow always loomed. He should have known how dark Colleen was, she had inflicted enough injuries on him. He should have reported her, taken the photographs to the police, instead of harbouring the secret, documenting it, to use against her for money. She may have got a custodial sentence, and he may have got control of the business. High insight. Dangerous to sanity. His greed was Daisy's death warrant. This whole situation was his punishment for that. He could have stopped all of this. His thoughts seemed to go around in circles, and the question that he always came back to was, who killed Colleen?

SHERRY

Sherry awoke with the rain pounding at her bedroom window. It sounded as though it would shatter the fragile old glass. She checked her watch, it was 5am and still dark. Her mood felt bleak, she hoped to awaken more upbeat, but she could already tell it would be another gloomy day.

She touched the picture of Dan in the frame beside her bed, and sighed, longing for the day when they could be together. He was still writing regularly, without any depth, but still, why would he bother at all if he didn't care?

He would have nothing when he eventually got out, and by then her property would have increased in value enough for them to sell it and move. They could

149

go abroad, where no one knew of them, and begin again. He would be forever in her debt for keeping him going through the years, and then organising his new life. It would likely be too late for any children, but that was good. They didn't need whining and selfish kids to taint their new-found happiness…just each other. A warm feeling of hope and longing crept over her, and gently pushed a little of the gloom away. She imagined he would feel the same about her, once he got over losing Daisy. She could wait. It would be worth it.

She hadn't bothered to visit Joan since the memorial service. Her energy was wasted in *that* direction, and there would be no more offers of help. She could hobble off and do her own shopping, irritating old bag.

Full packets of medication sat on her dressing table and reminded her that she had not taken any for a while. How long, she wasn't sure. But it was going ok, and she was coping well, weaning off them was always her intention, and it would be so amazing if Dan could get to know the real her. Not the sedate, boring Sherry, numb to the world. Hopping out of bed, she pulled open her drawer and slid the packets into it, out of sight. "Better."

Her phone beeped and she wearily reached across to read it, expecting a junk text as she so seldom received messages. Who was there to message her? Her family were lost, they had never believed in her. Always thought her unworthy of love. Friends seemed to have slipped away, she could understand to some extent, considering what went on, but real friends stood by you didn't they?

The message simply said: **Grass. You should have kept your mouth shut**.

Sherry sat on the edge of her bed and grappled with the phone to re-read the text, wiping sleep from her eyes. The number was unknown. At first her brain failed to make sense of what it could mean. Then, it dawned on her, Biker Guy.

How did they get her number? How did they know she spoke to the police? Her mind flashed to that first day when she witnessed Colleen and him out in the copse, perhaps he had seen her after all? Then something drew her to her linen cupboard on the landing. Folded neatly was a white t-shirt, stained with orange juice and blood, she stepped out of her pyjamas, and slipped it over her naked body. She lifted the newspaper article, which she had cut out, and realised that she had given her own game away:

"I have told the police that when I first moved here, I witnessed Colleen and a biker guy, (leathers and all the gear,) in woodlands beside my home. I didn't know who the lady was then, not until I met her again at their shop. They appeared to be having an altercation, and I guess now, it must have been the people who were blackmailing her. He also came into the shop asking for Dan, so I guess they both knew him. I have already identified this man to the police, like a photo-fit type thing."

Sherry took a deep breath and exhaled. Why couldn't she keep her mouth shut? Now she was on their radar and who knew what they were capable of. She had no money to bribe them with and although she did not frighten easily, this was not an ideal situation. She felt her way through her clothes into the back of the built-in wardrobe and retrieved a baseball bat, which she gently placed beside her bed. Then she took off the t-shirt, carefully folded it back up, placed it on the shelf, and shut the cupboard. She needed a coffee, and yawned her way downstairs, hoping her milk had not gone off.

It already felt like lunchtime and was only 10am. Getting up at 5am did that to you, and to combat the fatigue she decided to venture out for a walk through the woodland at the back. She grabbed her trainers and locked the back door, putting the rusty old key under the stone Buddha by the old outdoor privy, which was now more like a pile of crumbling bricks. The rickety old bench was on its last legs too and groaned beneath her weight as she tied her laces up. It was beyond repair and would need smashing up and replacing at some point.

She headed out of her secret gate. She still thought of it as a secret gate, because of the way it sat in the hedge and bushes. It wasn't really a secret, subtle was a more accurate description. The woods felt deserted, and she yomped over tree roots and tumps aimlessly, breathing in the fresh autumn air.

Except for distant cockerels and a peacock calling, it felt eerily quiet, as though she were the last person on earth. Her feet continued to roam without instruction and before she knew it, she was behind the trees outside Dan's. There was no bustling, or activity. It was like a ghost house, without movement, except for remnants of police tape flapping in the breeze. She stopped and lurked behind a huge oak, checking to see if anyone else was around, before silently sprinting along the side perimeter to the copse at the back of the property.

The resident peacock strutted, oblivious to her arrival, calling and spreading his beautifully ornate tail. Sherry dropped to her knees and crawled through the gap between two conifer trees into the thicket, and her eye immediately drew to a disturbed patch of ground. "Daisy, this was where she buried you?"

She stood beside the earth and looked towards the house. Although it was a fair distance away, she shook her head in disbelief, that poor Dan would have looked on this spot from every window he used at the back of the house. And Colleen would have carried on her life, frolicking in the hot tub, knowing exactly what she had done. What a callous bitch.

The hot tub was no longer in use and so the property was quiet. Before, the drone of the tub was a constant, and it seemed strange now it was off. Of course, it would have been forensically examined and drained, and who would ever want to get into a hot tub where someone died? She shivered. She better not risk going any closer in case they had the cameras working again. There was no way of explaining why she should be there, so she hovered for a moment longer and then soundlessly disappeared back through the thicket.

DAN

Miles was visiting. He had news. Potentially important and surprising.   Dan could not settle awaiting his arrival. Intrigued, an idea occurred which never had done before. Sherry. What if Sherry killed Colleen? The original Sherry, the person who he thought she was in the early days, was not capable. But this new person, who he was being fed information about, who was lying to him about Smokey and Jackie...who refused references. She seemed like a stranger he did not know, and maybe, therefore, capable of it? But why? What was her motive? Colleen pissed most people off on a daily basis, locally, and had more than likely been vile to Sherry in the shop, but murder? It didn't make complete sense, but perhaps he was on to something.

It was gone one when Miles arrived, and Dan was led from his cell to the meeting. It was good to see someone other than uniforms or grey tracksuits.

"Dan!" Mile's hair, usually in a smart quiff, was messy, and although he wore smart trousers and a shirt, his tie was missing. He was animated and energised.

"Miles. What you got for me?"

Miles rubbed his hands and beamed, "A whole can of worms it would seem. I hope you're ready?"

The hairs on the back of Dan's neck stood on edge as he settled as best as he could, in the solid plastic chair, designed purely for practicality over comfort. "Ready."

"Well, our Sherry, seems to have, somewhat, of a shady past...stalking for one."

"What? Stalking?" His eyes widened and his mouth hung open. He leaned onto the table, "Go on."

"It appears three separate injunctions have been taken out against her, with a husband and wife, and a separate individual. Quite renowned in the area of Exeter as a bit of a hatchet job. Has skipped her psychiatry sessions, not checked in for her meds review with her mental health team, or picked up any of her prescribed drugs since she arrived here. Don't ask me how I found all of this out, because it isn't strictly by the book. I need to do some more work on 'official' sources."

"Fuck. She seemed the opposite of everything you have described. I am fucking lost for words."

"Also, the wife, whom was part of an injunction, was threatened by her. Threatened with violence on multiple occasions. But never touched her, more intimidation. They suspected that she was wandering their property, so installed cameras, but she was sneaky enough to avoid them."

"I'm struggling to take all this in and what it could mean for us. Fuck."

"Well, it puts someone else in the picture. Because she told the Police a different story. They were aware that she had suffered with mental health issues, she told them about that, that she had been sectioned in the past and was on medication. But she did not reveal about the stalking. And that is because she used a different name. Her name is Michelle, not Sherry."

Dan could not comprehend the words Miles was saying. He put his palms towards him, "Stop, for one minute."

Miles shuffled his paperwork and swept his unruly hair into the resemblance of a quiff. "This is good."

Dan nodded. "It's a lot. So do you think…"

"That *she* did it? YES! I do. You, unfortunately, made it hard on yourself, because of your fight with Colleen, the injuries. But if we put this information together, and create a case, I think the police will have to consider her a suspect. The important thing is that she mustn't know we are at all suspicious of her. We must keep a lid on it. She is clever, and slippery. We don't want to lose any potential evidence. What we need really is a warrant for her arrest. So, I am going to put together everything I have found, jiggle it about, so it is all by the book, we don't want anything dismissed. If we pull this off, you will be up for blackmail charges and actual bodily harm, although you have a file of your own injuries, which will be a great source in your case. We could plead self-defence."

SHERRY

It was a painfully quiet Monday evening, and Jackie sent Sherry home at 9pm, earlier than usual. It was a waste of an evening, as Jackie had her folding napkins and polishing glasses, like a teenager working a Saturday job. It was a relief when she sent her home, an escape from the endless menial tasks.

She called in and bought a bottle of wine, as she passed the shop, to have with her cheese and crackers for supper. Everything seemed normal, until she got through her iron gate, and to the front door. It was open, and for a second she berated herself for being so careless. It wasn't the first time she had been lapse with security, she often forgot to lock the back door. But the front, didn't actually need locking, you just pulled it shut. She listened for a moment, and then pushed on in, closing the door behind her. A rumbling tummy begged for supper, she put a plate together, poured a large glass of red wine and settled on the sofa.

The evening birdsong was in full chorus, and she switched on the tv to drown it out. Sometimes she wished she could shoot them all, anything to shut them up. Her phone rang, she hoped it might be Dan, and jumped up, spilling red wine all over the floor. "For fucks sake." The phone stopped ringing as she reached it, and then began to ring again. "Hello!" She hoped she sounded enthusiastic rather than annoyed, Dan needed a cheerful, supportive chat, not a pissed off voice.

The line was silent, "Hellooo? Is that you Dan?"
Nothing. She ended the call, and it immediately rang
again. "Who is this?"

No one spoke. "Fuck off whoever this is." But it rang
again as soon as she ended the call. She switched the
phone off, throwing it onto the worn sofa cushion and
began to soak up the wine, which pooled on the
floorboards.

A shiver crept across her body. Little unnerved her,
but she was shaken as she locked the back door, and
then rechecked the front, bolting it top and bottom.
Unease built and her eyes scanned the room, but
nothing seemed out of place. Same in the kitchen and
bathroom. One step at a time she climbed the stairs,
slowly and quietly, listening for any sound or
movement. She paused outside her bedroom, her
brain flashing images of a balaclava-wearing intruder
awaiting her arrival. She blinked it away as her
shaking hands pushed open the door, and she stepped
inside. Nothing untoward caught her attention, no
masked invader lay waiting after all, and she breathed
a deep sigh of relief. Perhaps she was finally losing her
mind. She was always being told that she was
'unhinged' or 'crazy', until this moment, she had never
entertained it as a possibility. But as she remembered

the phone calls, she noticed her baseball bat was gone. Instinct drew her to the window, as though her subconscious hoped to catch a glimpse of the fleeing intruder, but of course there was no one to be seen, and she was left alone, knowing a stranger had been through her house.

She leaned against the window, shaking her head, what the fuck was going on? It was biker man and his lot. Her newspaper article was the dumbest thing she had ever done. She smacked at her forehead with her hand and checked under the bed, in case the bat had fallen over. It was gone. She would need alternative protection now and headed downstairs to find a knife. Passing her linen cupboard, she checked her items were all in place, and then locked the door and slipped the key into her pocket, kissing her fingers and pressing them to the door for a moment.

DAN

Dan pondered whether it had been a good idea to involve Miles with the others, but he would at least be making it clear that he was not part of Sherry's grassing. Miles would feed back the real identity of Sherry to them, and this was message enough. They would understand whose side he sat on. He decided that he was at peace with this choice, and it may offer him some security, as he was all too aware, that prison offered no protection from those types. And he could not deny he felt vulnerable. He was still using his anger to fuel a fitness mission, and figured the bulkier he was, the more chance he stood if they decided to come for him.

Sherry seemed to be haunting him, and his stomach turned every time a letter arrived, and he drafted back some lame reply. Miles was adamant that she must think everything was the same, and so contact was vital. He managed to keep her away from visiting, he knew he could never pretend across the table in person, he would want to ring her neck. Fucks sake hadn't there been enough of that already, he berated himself for thinking that way. It was still incredible that both Daisy and Colleen were dead. These things happened on the telly, in some Netflix crime documentary, not in the countryside in England, and not to him.

Joan was coming to visit; Jackie was bringing her. Top secretly of course, because Sherry could not know they were in contact. Miles had instructed him not to let them know anything, because if they let something slip out, it could jeopardise their case. But he would be glad to see a friendly face, and bathe in sympathetic words, that was enough for now. Especially as there was light at the end of the tunnel.

Joan looked frail and compact, and she gave him a little wave as he rounded the corner. Her usual bravado and steel seemed to have buckled amidst the prison setting, as she stood to hug him. But she still wore her beige mac. It was nice to see something so familiar.

"You don't look half as bad as I was thinking."

"Thanks, not much to do in here Joan, so have kept busy with exercises."

"It's so good to see you." Her mouth smiled through her tears.

"Don't get upset, I'm okay."

"You shouldn't be in here."

Dan squeezed her hand. "I have a good brief. Don't worry about me. Now tell me how you are?"

Joan removed a handkerchief from her mac pocket and wiped her tears away. "I told you she was a wrong 'un, didn't I, when she first arrived."

Dan nodded. "Sherry, you mean?"

"Yep. She is unrecognisable Dan. It's like she has shed her skin and is somebody new."

Dan's mind flashed the image of a snake. "She is certainly trying to keep anyone from contacting me."

"I think she is obsessed with you. She wants to be your world, make you rely on her alone, think she is the only one who cares..."

Dan thought about everything that Miles had discovered. That was her motive. She killed Colleen because of him. She wanted him for herself. But why then let him rot in prison?

"You know I didn't kill her, don't you?"

"You asking me that? Of course, I know, wouldn't be here otherwise, would I? Not up for being friends with a murderer. Jackie's still got her working at the pub.

But the regulars don't like her at all and are not going in when she is there. So, she's having to give her other, less customer orientated jobs to work on, and it isn't going down well. But what else can Jackie do? I mean, she wants to keep an eye on her, see if she says anything that could help you at all. Jackie thinks she knows something about Colleen."

Dan paused, considering his answer carefully. His friends were going all out for him, but they could be in danger, she was dangerous. They had no idea how much of a liability she was. "I think Jackie should ask her to leave. I don't want her to mess with their business, and I don't want you to go near her either. You must give her a wide berth."

"But…"

"Joan, I know you both care about me, and if you really do, then promise me, you will cut her off. You can easily find an excuse; she doesn't know we are in contact. She will love that, anyway, feeling like she is carrying the flag alone. But you must speak to Jackie and tell her to lay her off straight away. And you, well, don't let her in the house and don't go near her."

Joan frowned and sighed. A moment of silence weighed down on them both. Dan had probably said too much, and Joan, he guessed was reluctant to promise.

Eventually she nodded. "Aye, I promise, although I don't understand why. But I also know not to ask you anything more."

SHERRY

Sherry ran in through the pub door and hung up her wet coat to dry near the fire. It had rained for two days. The pub was empty, but it was still early. Jackie and Smokey stood behind the bar, as though awaiting her arrival.

Smokey remained silent but lingered as Jackie spoke. "This is for you." She pushed a small brown wages envelope across the bar. "It's your wages up to today, and I have divvied up the tips too, so they are included."

"Isn't it a bit early for payday?" Sherry chewed her lip and scowled. This was her marching orders, but she wasn't going to make it easy on them.

"Sorry, but we just can't afford to keep you on. You must see how quiet it is lately."

That's because it's a shithole, she wanted to say. Because you and Smokey are the most boring people I have ever met, and the food is overpriced and underwhelming. But instead, she replied, "Of course, but I thought you wanted to help me? I really thought I was doing a good job Jackie. All those glasses I've polished, and napkins I have folded."

Smokey stepped forward, obviously picking up on her sarcasm, but Jackie pushed him covertly back. "You've been great, a real help. But business is business, and we cannot afford to keep you on. So, with thanks, please take your wages and have a drink on us. No hard feelings. Eh? Vodka and coke?"

Sherry nodded and slipped the wages into her pocket. She was uneasy about what was going on, and wondered how genuine this termination of employment was. Perhaps Joan had been spouting off about her, she was such a fucking busy body. She swiped the drink from the bar and lifted it up to her ex-employers. "Cheers." At least she had another sob-story to provoke Dan's sympathy. Being ostracised by the village because of him, and the job was dull as shit anyway. Maybe it was for the best.

"Right. That's that then guys!" She drained the last of her drink and slammed the glass on the bar. "I'll leave you to it then." Her coat was still dripping wet as she put it on, but the rain outside was subsiding. Perhaps she would take a slight detour via Joans, now the rain was easing off. Maybe she had something to say about the pub, and her dismissal.

She pushed through the whining gate, along Joans path, and slammed the heavy knocker against the door. She waited for a moment, before repeating it and then shouted, "Joan, are you in there?" through the letterbox. She pushed her face against the window and squinted, trying to see through the crisp white lace of the net curtain. But detected no movement inside. She was too clever, avoiding her no doubt. Her fist pounded the window, and then returned to hammering the knocker. "It's only Sherry, Joan, open up!"

After a few moments, she stood still and listened, convinced of a muffled shuffling in the house, but without breaking down the door, she could not prove her theory one way or the other. She headed back up the path, glancing back over her shoulder, hoping to catch a twitching of net curtains. Sneaky Joan, hiding from her. What she didn't realise was this only fired up her idea that Joan had a hand in her losing her job, because otherwise why wouldn't she open the door to her?

The light rain suddenly became heavy, and within seconds Sherry was drenched. Her hair dripped over her face, streaking her make up, and her clothing stuck to her skin. She jogged towards home, desperate to remove her sodden clothes and get in a hot shower.

Almost home, she turned the corner onto her road, and a lorry came speeding towards her. As it hit the puddle she gasped. The wave of water splashed her, covering her face and body with mud. She screamed, her anger consuming her," You fucking idiot! Go fuck yourself you utter prick!" She stooped and picked up a discarded coke can and threw it after the lorry.

Limping soggily home, she stripped off just inside the door, throwing her clothes into the kitchen sink before taking a shower.

As she towel-dried her hair, she checked her phone. There had been no more weird phone calls, thankfully, because she couldn't call the police about it. She needed as little contact with them as possible, in fact she was aiming to fade from their peripheral.   She lifted her pillow and sighed, her knife was still there, and offered her only protection since they had taken her baseball bat. They would only be frightening her; intimidation was their game, like she first witnessed that day in the woods with Colleen.

 She pressed a kiss onto the linen cupboard door as she passed and headed downstairs to sort out her sodden clothes. Moving through the hallway, towards the kitchen, an envelope hanging from the letterbox caught her eye. The name written on the front, rooted her to the spot. She stared at the bold capital letters, which spelled out MICHELLE, and her stomach churned as she fought the urge to tear it into pieces. Slumping to the floor onto her knees, she banged her shoulder, rhythmically into the wall. Everything had changed now, and she needed to make some quick decisions.

DAN

Miles was getting somewhere, and confident he had a case to take to the police. Any day he expected to be called back into the interview room, for re-opening of the investigation. They were pretty pissed off and concerned that this would make them appear incompetent initially, having only followed the circumstantial evidence. Dan hoped he wouldn't be convicted anyway, amidst a police-force cover up. Sherry's contact was less and less. Jackie and Joan wrote to him, describing how they had carried out his wish, and cut her off. But he sensed a much more serious reason for her quietness. Miles having managed to contact *them* and give *them* intel on her real name and history, she would be busy fighting that fire, he imagined.

Anticipation was building, even though he tried to keep it in check, in case it all went tits up again. Miles seemed fired up and was not going to give up easily. His door swung open. He sat up, and watched as the burly, tattooed bloke hurtled towards him, stopping only once Dan's arm was twisted up behind his back. It was at that moment he realised, the hours he spent doing press ups were futile and he did not stand a chance.

"Been asked to pay you a visit."

Dan winced as his elbow felt close to snapping.

"Boss wants you to know, that your bit on the side begged for your baby's life. Reckons your crazy wife wouldn't have killed her, if she hadn't found out about the baby. Only wanted to frighten her off. Your Mrs spilled her guts while they dug your dead girlfriend into the ground. Covered in dirt, she rambled on about how she lost her shit, and couldn't stop." He tightened his grip, but Dan didn't care, his mind was busy picturing Daisy laying on his patio.

"Boss knows you didn't grass. Keep it that way. As long as you keep quiet, our dealing is done. You have nothing more worth anything to us."

Dan nodded slowly. "I understand. I've said nothing and will say nothing."

"If you had, you wouldn't be stood here now. You would've been sorted out the moment you hit this wing." He pushed Dan hard against the wall, and by the time Dan got his balance and turned he was gone.

His arm was agony, but his imagination tortured him: Colleen stood in front of Daisy, who begged for her child's life, not realising that that would be her death warrant. He was glad Colleen was dead.

If it wasn't for her, he and Daisy would be married by now, well maybe not married, Colleen would never have given him a divorce, but together. Their baby born, they would be doting parents, loving it. Happy. A tear blurred his eye, but he wiped it away. "Not yet. No time for that yet."

He hopped to the floor, and pushed through the arm pain as he began his press-ups. This time he was doing it for himself. He didn't need it for protection, it was for his own sanity. To work off his anger and keep his head in the game. He still had a battle to fight, to win if he wanted any sort of life.

Sherry, now to be known as Michelle, needed to be taken down, made to pay for everything she had put him through. For murdering Colleen, and for the lies and deceit she had maintained so easily for so long. Michelle would pay, and that was his sole focus from now on.

MICHELLE

Michelle knew she couldn't take everything. It was a quick evacuation rather than an official house move. Every moment she stayed, upped the danger she was in. *They* knew who she was, and that meant also about her past. How long before everyone else did too? Sporadically running from room to room, she threw items into black bags and then hastily loaded them into her car, which she had pulled up to the pavement immediately outside her front gate. Her mind was scrambled, and she struggled to think straight, the evidence of which was the random chosen possessions sat in her car. How different this move was, compared to the day she arrived. A pang of sadness washed over her, and her eyes filled with tears. Why did her life always end up in such a mess?

She took a deep breath and checked her watch, it was almost 7pm. She reached into her pocket for her key and sprinted upstairs to the linen cupboard, which she began to pile up and then put carefully into her rucksack. She had quite a decent collection this time, including a lock of red hair, which she wrapped gently in a length of loo roll and then tucked into the inside pocket of the bag. As she zipped up the rucksack, her front door slammed and she froze, holding the bag tight into her chest.

Heavy footsteps came closer, and she was cornered with no escape. Was it the Police? Was it *them*? Her legs threatened to run, but there was nowhere to go, and her breath sounded like it was being played through an amplifier. She was sure whoever it was, would be able to hear her breathing and clamped her hand over her mouth. No face appeared at the bottom of the staircase, so slowly and as quietly as she could manage, she crept backwards, up the top few stairs, into her room and climbed into her still-full wardrobe, pulling the door closed. Crouched in a ball, her mind swam with tangled thoughts. This could be her moment to die, perhaps this messy thinking, was her version of life flashing before her.

It felt like hours before the footsteps entered her room. She could tell there was at least two people, and her knife, was still under her pillow, so she had nothing with which to protect herself. Perhaps the clothes would hide her, and they would only glance in the wardrobe. Who was she kidding, this wasn't fucking Narnia.

The door flung open, and before she even registered what happened, they yanked her out and threw her on the bed, a knee to her chest.

"Here she is, hiding away like a scared little mouse. You must be Sherry, or should we say, Michelle?"

They weren't the Police, there was no uniforms. They were dressed normally, inconspicuously except for surgical masks, to scramble their features. That was positive, maybe they weren't going to kill her after all, otherwise why cover their faces?

"What do you want from me? What I told the Police, was nothing really. I mean, what do I know anyway? Just a face I saw, apart from that I have nothing worth telling."

Whilst she spoke her wrists and ankles were bound. Her only route out now, was her words and her mind was all over the place. "What are you going to do with me? I'm small fry, surely? Dan has more on you than me, its him I would be more concerned with."

The larger of the two, rolled her onto the floor and began kicking her. "Shut the fuck up."

Pain ricocheted through her body with each new blow, and she knew this was her end. She was at their mercy. She had no one. No one to miss her, probably wouldn't be found for days or weeks. Her mind lifted her up above her body and she watched the incessant beating, as her face bloodied, and her bound hands fought to protect her now swollen, face. Then she floated away, and there was nothing.

DAN

This time, he was seated back in an uncomfortable plastic chair, beneath another harsh strip light, awaiting Miles. The interview room was as grim as the first and it even had its own smudges across the two-way mirror. Miles was never late, and usually, he wasn't brought out of his cell until he arrived. Perhaps he was already in the building but talking to someone. He chewed on his already bleeding thumb nail.

The door opened and Miles was followed in by Trent and Burton. "Can I have a word with my client before we begin?"

"Two minutes." Burton left the room with Trent in tow.

"Miles, what's going on?"

"They almost killed her. The police went to arrest her, bring her in for questioning, two more minutes and they would have been too late."

"She's not dead?"

"No, but she's in a bad way."

"Did they get away? Did the police catch them?"

"No, they had scooters out the back in the woods, according to a witness. Long gone by the time they found them ditched, a few miles out."

"Where does that leave us, me?"

The door opened, and Trent and Burton re-entered the room, looking pale and nervy.

The interview commenced, with a fresh angle. Sherry, they wanted to know about Sherry, Michelle.

"What did you know about Michelle Greaves when she approached you for a job?"

"Nothing, we chatted, she seemed nice, and I was desperate to be honest, so thought I would give her a chance."

"And you didn't think to get any references, previous work history, where she even came from?"

"I approached her about references, but it kind of got swept under the carpet, events took hold and I guess I got distracted."

"How often did you visit her?"

"A couple of times, never stayed long."

"And how many times did she visit you?"

"Never. She never came to our house."

The two officers looked at one another, they appeared confused.

"There was a short-cut, through the woods?"

"Yes, I went home that way once. I'd been to the pub, she made me coffee and I left through the back gate, across the woodland path. What, do you think she'd been sneaking around? Fucking hell."

"We know now that she has a history of stalking, probably quite used to avoiding cameras, from what little we know. We are trawling through the one camera which was working, behind your office, this one was left on, never threw anything of use up when we investigated Daisy's murder, but now we are looking to place Michelle Greaves at your property. And finding her on camera, even for a second, would be useful. Of course, we have other evidence, which would be impossible for her to explain away."

"So, do you think maybe she was there, when me and Col were fighting? Watching? Everything?" He shuddered and his skin crawled.

"Anything is possible. It seems she has not been taking medication which keeps her stable. We found a bag of it at her house."

"As Michelle is still unconscious, and you cannot interview her, will you be able to drop the charges of murder?"

"You are no longer interviewing my client on murder charges, for the record, this is a witness interview." Miles was using his most stern voice.

Burton reluctantly nodded. "Charges have been dropped, but you are still up for blackmail, a serious offence, and we also have the assault to consider. You aren't off the hook here. It's still magistrates court for you."

"We have the counter evidence, that in fact my client was a victim of domestic abuse himself, this whole case needs to be re-evaluated."

Burton nodded and cleared his throat.

"I have to say, we, both my client and I, have been uncomfortable with the way this was conducted since the beginning, you can expect a complaint from us." Miles stared at the paling officers.

"I want the truth. I want to get out of this place. I told you from the start, I didn't do it." Dan stood.

"Sit down Dan. Considering this new information, we will be reviewing the case, and will lead further investigations. But do not expect to be getting out any time soon – you'll be behind bars for a long time to come."

Trent switched off the tape machine, and they solemnly left the room.

"My head is mashed Miles...blackmail, I didn't think it would be as serious as that. Fucks sake."

"You didn't think, that's the problem. Perhaps if you had thought more, you wouldn't have engaged in criminal activity, sorry Dan but you did this."

"But the murder charge is dropped..."

"She still had injuries. Injuries which you inflicted. You must answer to that too."

"But we have my photos, a history of abuse by her."

"They will ask, why you kept these and didn't report her. Although it isn't unusual for victims not to report their abuser."

"So, if Michelle makes it, they will interview and charge her?"

"That's about it."

"And if she doesn't?"

"Then they have enough evidence to pin it on her regardless, and you're still off the hook. For the murder at least."

"Fuck me!" Dan stood up and sat down again. He was wired. "I just can't take it in..."

"This is good Dan."

"Too fucking right, it's fucking amazing."

"But remember how serious blackmail is. You could be looking at 14 years."

"I don't think it will come to that. Surely? We can go for the sympathy vote, poor abused husband, trying to tip abuser over the edge…"

"Or maybe they will see it as: psychologically damaging husband drives wife to violence with black mail and infidelity."

Dan shot Miles a look of fury and it dawned on him, that he was still in deep shit.

MICHELLE

The body lying unconscious could have been anyone, it was initially unrecognisable. No visitors came to comfort her or offer words of encouragement to fight. Only a regular shift-change of two hopeful police officers, wondering if that day will be the one where she would speak.

There wasn't much point her fighting to come back, because what would she be coming back for? Interrogation, arrest, imprisonment. And yet, when her eyes opened and took their first furtive, weary glances around the clinically lit intensive care unit, she knew everything was different. And she wished she could have let go of the world that had only ever been mysterious, cruel and puzzling to her.

The familiar beep of the machines had been her constant since arriving at the hospital. Now she was plugged into fewer contraptions, she felt more human and less robot, but her throat was agony since the tubes had been removed, and she was yet to find her voice. She had a thirst which could not be quenched.

The doctors were the only thing preventing her from being questioned by the two figures who stood at her window daily; guarded her door. She knew that soon, there would be no intervention which could stop that.

Each day she felt her body healing, and the staff were constantly telling her how well she was doing. Her tears would fall and continue for hours sometimes. This was all normal according to the trauma nurses, a combination of her multiple injuries and medication. But she knew it was due to things other than that. For her, the kindness she was shown, the dignity which they ensured she kept, and the love they showered her with, was the greatest care she had ever known in her entire life. Never had she felt so important, been offered such concern, been reassured that she was

184

going to be ok. This was both her worst time and her most wonderful, all mushed together into a confusing tumble of thoughts and emotions.

Maeve was her favourite nurse. She always fussed around her. Whilst unconscious she could hear her kind voice, discussing how sad she was that she had no one, not a soul who cared enough to visit, and now she was awake, her support continued. People like her, made the world a better place.

Michelle was beginning to formulate what she would say to the police, they would have found her house half packed up, and her rucksack... There was no escaping the contents of that. The question was, should she spill her version, tell the truth, or lie, and lead them away from what happened, away from her?

Pain wracked her body, and she was thankful for the morphine they continued to pump her full of, despite the side effects of visual disturbances and muddled thoughts. Maeve had told her that there wasn't a patch on her body which was unbruised. Perhaps it was what she deserved for taking a life, even if the person deserved to die.

Her past was now her present, and there was no way out of that. She could feign memory loss, but they would prove her brain was not damaged, with all the scans she had undergone. So much for the fresh start she hoped for. When she moved to the village, she was genuinely optimistic that this was it. Sherry was born, a new improved version of Michelle. A decent, hard-working member of the community. Where had it all gone wrong?

Landing her job at Dan's, seemed like the golden ticket at the time. How could she have guessed, with all the lies he told, and the beautiful family run business he described, that behind the sage green façade and beautiful wicker baskets, was a volatile marriage; a web, hanging about, to ensnare unsuspecting arrivals. She could have made it work, if she had kept out of it, didn't let Colleen get under her skin. Her heart rate increased thinking about her. Vile, mean and rude.

Maeve's cheery humming broke Michelle's thoughts and she turned her head the minutest fraction her collared neck would allow. She winced at the tiny movement.

"Is that a little smile you are trying to give me?" Maeve brushed a loose strand of hair away from Michelle's eyes. "Perkier today! Time for me to give you a little wash and do some 'obs' on you, okay?"

Not much I could do about it anyway, Michelle thought, but she didn't mind and trusted Maeve, she had always been kind and as gentle as touching broken, bruised and split skin can be. It felt better once it was done anyway, refreshing, despite the pain.

"Thank you." She mouthed, her voice still missing in action.

"You're most welcome. While you're under my care, you can rest assured there is no judgement here...let's leave that up to the magistrate, eh?"

Michelle felt her cheeks blush. For the first time, she felt something new. This compassionate woman, who tirelessly cared for her, knowing what she was accused of, had provoked a disturbing new emotion in her. Awoken something, which no one had ever managed. Shame, and regret. Perhaps it was because she understood that the level of care she was receiving, was over and above what this nurse needed to deliver. She wanted her to be comfortable, clean and to heal. She wanted to give her the best care she could, even though she was aware she was accused of murder. Maybe she also understood that people aren't simply bad, or good. That good people are capable of bad deeds. And likewise, bad people can also do good for the world. Michelle was under no illusion which side of the fence she fell on. But what good deeds had she done in her life? She racked her brain, for a memory, of something selfless she did. And she could not remember doing anything good for anyone, which didn't have a motive.

Her breathing sped up with her frustration and anger, and every single movement caused her to silently scream out, as she pulled at tubes, and blood spilled over the white sheets which covered her battered body. She deserved none of this compassion. They should have let her die. Maeve smacked the alarm, and the room filled with scrubs, who pinned her down and then injected a sedative. Sleep came and rescued her from her waking darkness.

DAN

Dan mulled over the information Miles brought with him, on his most recent visit. He played the words around his mind, wondering if this could all be real.

"They found a rucksack in her wardrobe, full of stuff, pictures of you. Your mug from the shop and a blood-stained t-shirt with orange juice over it…"

It was so fucked up…he didn't know how to feel, and he rubbed his hair. Shaking his head, curling his face in disgust.

"That shirt was from when Colleen smashed a glass jug over my head. I put that into my bathroom bin…she must have been into my bedroom…" he had told Miles.

"The best thing, the absolute clincher, was wrapped in toilet paper, in the inside pocket of her bag. A tiny lock of red hair. Colleen's."

This creepy, fucked up collection Michelle had stowed away, was now the evidence which would free him from the murder charge. And still, his stomach churned. So much had changed, and yet he was still looking at a long stretch.

They had already offered him a deal if he spilled on who was assisting him with the blackmail, but he refused to give them anything. He wanted to stay alive, and if he said a word, he wouldn't see another sunrise. He would be carrying the can, alone. He might be out by the time he got to 50, if he was lucky. Miles was working hard to put together his defence, and he trusted him, but it was all a mess.

Michelle was awake and under constant police guard, she had been charged. He wondered if he would ever get a definitive answer, as to her reason for killing Colleen. Surely it wasn't because of how she felt for him? They were nothing more than work colleagues, acquaintances. His initial elation at murder charges being dropped, had worn off. What did it matter why you were in prison? Prison was prison, and blackmail was seen as serious as murder anyway. He was fucked. If Michelle hadn't murdered Colleen, he would not be rotting in prison now.

Victimhood was his protection, a safety-wall to hide behind, away from taking responsibility. Both Colleen and Michelle, had landed him behind bars. And fate was punishing them, for all they had done to him.

MICHELLE

Perpetual hell. No voice. Her damaged voice box was punishment for the lies she told so easily. Now she had no voice to use. The sight in her left eye was gone, and she lost her top front teeth, payment for her recent found vanity. There was always a price to pay for sin. She was a sinner. The hospital pumped her full of medication, and she was back to thinking more rationally. What the fuck had she done? She was still in bed, her broken body slowly knitting back together.

Flashes of her linen cupboard, and the items she had collected danced before her eyes, and despite her vision loss, they were clear and vivid. She shuddered. It was as though she had been possessed by someone else, because the recollection of what she had done was too much to accept as her own actions. How she expertly crept around the rooms of Dan's home, undetected. Snooping, listening, watching. Gathering items to treasure. How she sometimes watched the rise and fall of his chest as he slept, a riskier challenge, concerned he could wake and find her.

It was as though she had lived through a nightmare, and now she awoke, relieved it was over, only to find it was all real. Now that person was gone, and as always, she was left to pay the hefty price.

This time there would be no opportunity for a fresh start because she would forever carry around the label, of murderer. Her toothless, mashed up face, would be spewed across all the newspapers, and people would talk about their own encounters with 'Sherry', Michelle, and how they always knew there was something creepy about her.

Her name would be added to the Netflix list of fascinating crimes to document...perhaps they would request an interview. But she would decline, of course. Because that person, the one people saw, whispered about and shunned, wasn't the self she clung to. She spent her life barely gripping to the edge of who she really was, and yet the one she slipped into, when the medication wore off, was the infamous one. The one people wanted to read about and try and climb inside the mind of. Which she found bizarre, because she would do anything to be free of that persona.

Michelle watched the early sun stream through the blind, creating a pattern on the floor. Silently, she acknowledged the arrival of another day of hell.

It's scary what can happen, when we close our eyes to the truth.

WE CLOSE OUR EYES, by Sarah Colliver

I would like to thank those who continue to champion and encourage me, through my writing journey. It is easy to help someone who is already winning, but to lift and assist someone aiming high, is harder to do. So, to all of you, who share, recommend and review my words, THANK YOU. I would not have written this book without YOU.

My special thanks for extra support:

Elaine Malsom, Eleanor Cook, Melanie Maguire, Angharad Wrigley.

Sarah Colliver 2023

Printed in Great Britain
by Amazon

25969920R00116